3/9

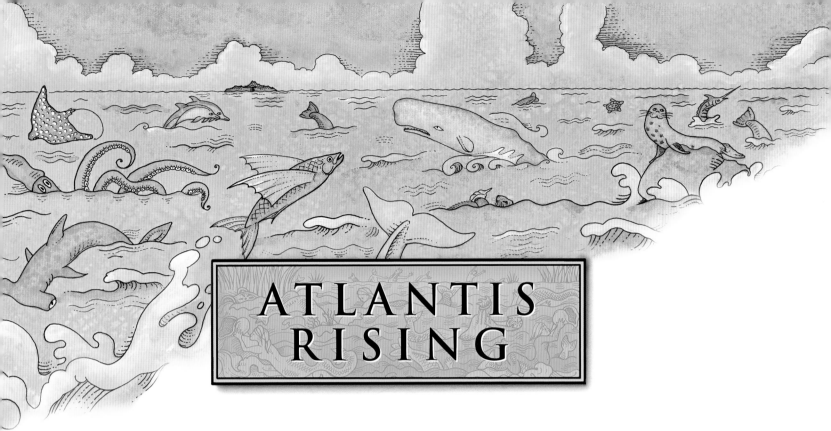

ATLANTIS RISING

THE TRUE STORY OF A SUBMERGED LAND
YESTERDAY AND TODAY

BY

ROBERT SULLIVAN

DRAWINGS BY

GLENN WOLFF

SIMON & SCHUSTER

Dedication

AD LUCILLAM ET CAROLINAM

AMOR SICUT MARE PROFUNDUS AETERNUSQUE SICUT

INSULA ATLANTIS

—R. S.

AD PATRICIAM MATREM

OLIM AUFUGACEM APUD CATERVAM MUSICARUM

—G. W.

CONTENTS

THE HERMIT BY THE BEACH
What Lurks Beneath These Waves?

"CALL ME ATWATER."

I had been expecting an alias, but no

alias in particular. I was instantly

amused by his cover, and I smiled

into the phone.

"Atwater?"

"Atwater. Call me Atwater."

"Well, Mr. Atwater…"

"Just Atwater."

"Fine. Atwater. Well, as I was saying, Atwater,

I've heard from a mutual friend that

you have some information."

"I have. Yes. I have information."

"About Atlantis?"

"About Atlantis. That is correct. I have some

good, solid information—certain information

about Atlantis."

HE CONTINUED: "And I have something else, besides information. Beyond information."

"What else could you have?" I was feeling whimsical. Perhaps he thought me arrogant or even insulting when I added, "What else could anyone possibly want, or possibly need, beyond certain information of Atlantis?"

"I have . . ." His voice was shaky throughout, and here it trailed off. Then it came back strong and direct. "I have photographs."

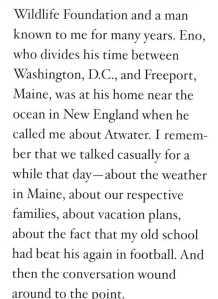

ATWATER WAS CALLING from a pay phone at a used-car lot somewhere on the eastern end of Cape Cod. It was sundown on an autumn afternoon, and he was calling at precisely the arranged time.

I would never have found Atwater, certainly would never have given any credence at all to an "Atwater" character, had I not been put on to him by a source of impeccable integrity, high standing and great seriousness. My contact was Amos S. Eno, executive director of the National Fish and Wildlife Foundation and a man known to me for many years. Eno, who divides his time between Washington, D.C., and Freeport, Maine, was at his home near the ocean in New England when he called me about Atwater. I remember that we talked casually for a while that day—about the weather in Maine, about our respective families, about vacation plans, about the fact that my old school had beat his again in football. And then the conversation wound around to the point.

Amos S. Eno, executive director, National Fish and Wildlife Foundation

"I hear," said Eno, "that you're looking into Atlantis."

"Starting to," I acknowledged. "It might even make a book. How did you hear?"

"I can't remember who told me," he said with some unease. "I just heard." I wondered at this. *How* had he *just heard?*

"Well, it's a fascinating topic," I said. "Volcanoes, mythology, legend, mystery, good-and-evil—it's got it all, that's for sure."

"Yes," said Eno. "Maybe more, too."

"More than all?" I asked.

"Could be," said Eno.

"How could it have more than all?"

"Well," he said. "It could be true."

This didn't surprise me. "Some have always said that," I replied mildly. "Plato believed in it, and ever since . . ."

Amos interrupted, which was not his way. "There's something else," he said.

"Tell me."

"Well," he said, considering. "Well, it could still be out there. Down there. I know a guy who says . . ."

"Wait a second," I said, interrupting in turn. "You're telling me that Atlantis not only might have happened, but that it still exists? What's going

FROM A PHONE AT THE
USED-CAR LOT, ATWATER SAID,
"I HAVE SOMETHING BESIDES
INFORMATION."
HE SAID HE HAD PROOF.

"This is what some people believe," he reiterated with, I sensed, questionable conviction.

"Nonsense!" I said. "People believe in lots of crazy things. It's nuts! Look at Roswell, New Mexico. It's nonsense!"

"It's not. Atlantis is not just another Roswell."

"It's crazy, I tell you. Nuts. I can't imagine anyone who would . . ."

"I believe it," my friend Amos Eno said suddenly. "I believe in Atlantis."

"You don't."

"I do. And I can put you in touch with a man."

on here, Amos? Is there a dig happening? Someone's going to excavate? Is someone going after it, like with the *Titanic*? I want to be there. Who do I call?"

"No, no, no," he said. "Listen, and listen carefully. What I'm saying is this: There are people who believe, who claim to have evidence in their possession, that Atlantis not only exists, but that Atlantis thrives." He paused to let this sink in, but I still didn't get it. "They believe there are Atlanteans," he continued finally. "Today. Alive. Atlanteans. It is not a remnant population, but a burgeoning race that has grown and evolved since The Cataclysm. There are hundreds of thousands of them if not millions of them. Some are undersea dwellers, sea mammals as closely related to whales or seals or manatees as they are to man. And then some in the older generations are still vaguely amphibian.

Atwater

AND SO I learned of Atwater. And so, a few weeks thereafter, I was receiving an early-evening phone call from a quiet spot somewhere on the eastern end of the peninsula that is Cape Cod, Massachusetts.

By the time I took that strange call, Amos had already told me a bit about this Atwater. Atwater was smart, Amos had said. He was scared. He felt that he was on the run, even if it was unclear that anyone at all was chasing him. One thing was certain: He was in possession of some very hot property.

ATWATER had grown up on an island in Puget Sound, one of the San Juan Islands that draw flocks of tourists to the Pacific Northwest these days, but that were lonely, rocky, big-pine outposts of considerable desolation when Atwater had been a boy. If the islands have forever been rough-hewn, they have also been eternally beautiful. Atwater loved them. He loved the Sound, and, beyond its wide mouth, he loved the great expansive ocean. He became a deft hand at sailing, and an expert on local flora and fauna; precociously, he drew his own natural history books. By the time he was of an age to leave those islands for the mainland, he was so tied to the proliferous populations of bald eagles, harbor seals and orcas that he felt he was leaving behind not only human but extra-human family and friends.

But leave he did, for he was intelligent, and to stay would have been to stifle. He went to school in the West, and—no surprise to those who knew him—he studied oceanography. He was tops in his class, and upon graduating he landed a job at the nation's most prestigious oceanographic institute,

Atwater trusted me to the degree that he shared images of Atlantis, and a few of himself.

Woods Hole Research Institute, Woods Hole, Massachusetts

the one at Woods Hole, Massachusetts. There he would work with and learn from the legends, from George Woodwell and Woodwell's associates. There he would come to know all there was to know about marine life, and he would seek to improve the ecological prospects of the sea around us.

He spent more than two decades engaged in these efforts. Amos Eno, in his work first at the Audubon Society and then at the Foundation, came to know and respect Atwater during this time. They took birding trips together, and went on whale-counting expeditions in the North Atlantic. Atwater became something of an uncle to Amos and Marjorie Eno's two children.

And then, one day not very long ago, Atwater didn't show up for work. No one in or around Woods Hole has seen him since.

Why?

"BECAUSE I KNEW too much," Atwater told me when we met. He said it matter-of-factly, with no unnecessary drama. "I had learned too much, and they were starting to get concerned that I would tell." He knit his fingers, leaned forward in the chair. "They were right to be concerned." There was a certain tension, surely, but his voice was firm and even.

We were sitting in a gray-shingled shack on the property of Pammy and Craig Beaver in the village of Truro. Upon Craig Beaver's retirement as a magazine editor in New York, the couple had relocated to Cape Cod. They now lived year-round just across the meadow in a great house hard by the water, in the crook—on the bay side—of the Cape's elbow. The Beavers rented their small, weather-beaten outbuilding for enormous sums from June to September, and for whatever they could get, when they could get anything at all, during the off-season. Two weeks prior to my meeting with him, Atwater had come knocking on the Beavers' door. In short order he had secured the shack for a month. He had packed in his few possessions, his files and his photographs.

He was, in fact, less than an hour's drive from Woods Hole, but the Cape is a hollow, windswept, lonesome place in autumn. You can blend in, like a tiger cat amidst the fallen gold and orange leaves. For now, at least, Atwater would hide in plain sight.

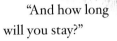

PLAIN SIGHT was at the end of North Pamet Road, between a small pond and a cranberry bog that had been left uncultivated for years. Atwater had given me directions, and had greeted me at the door without presumption or, as I've said, any hint of nervousness. He was a fit man of perhaps fifty-five years, clean-shaven and cleanly coiffed. He did not look the eccentric.

We shook hands, then sat inside sipping tea and gaining our ease for perhaps an hour. He mentioned that "they" were right to be concerned about him, and then said, "Let's go take a walk. Let's go talk of Atlantis."

Did he want to do this outside for any particular reason? I wondered.

"There's a path through the bog," he said, leading the way. "It's tranquil there. Lovely, serene, quiet." The worn boardwalk wound through overgrowth of gorse and bearberry; the smell of cranberry sweetened the moist fall air. "Beaver tells me there was cranberrying here from the 1800s till 1962," said Atwater. "All things must pass, I guess."

"How long have you been out here?" I asked.

"A very short time," he said. "Two weeks."

"And how long will you stay?"

"No telling," he said. "It's up to them. It depends how they react."

"They? The Beavers?"

"No. The folks at the Institute. It depends on them. How hard will they try to find me? Are they worried? Do they even care?"

"About . . ."

"About Atlantis. About The Atlantis Project. About knowledge getting out."

"You're talking in riddles. Are you trying to be cryptic here? Amos told me that you were a pretty straightforward guy."

He stopped on the planking just before the walkway climbed into a range of large sand dunes. He turned, and even in the dusk I could tell that his gaze was firm, unwavering; it made me more than a little bit uncomfortable. "I used to be, always," said Atwater. "Straightforward, always. Clinical. Scientific.

"But," he continued, "this Atlantis stuff has me very, very confused."

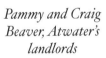

Pammy and Craig Beaver, Atwater's landlords

WE TRUDGED to the crest of the mighty dunes that front the ocean, dunes that were pure New England in aspect on their inland side, stitched together as they were by sea grass, but then tan and Arabic on the ocean side, where the sand flowed down to the surf. "What was Atlantis?" I asked. I felt I knew, but wanted to hear it from him.

"Before the volcano?"

"Yes."

"It was an island, of course. Not quite a continent, though many have called it that—'the lost continent.'

"It was an island in the Aegean Sea about seventy miles north of the larger island of Crete. The name for what remains of this island is Thera—Thera or Santorini. The old myth is that a local god named Triton gave the Argonauts a clump of earth which they dropped into the sea, forming Santorini—or Atlantis. That's a nice story, a nice mythical story. I figure it was, in geological fact, formed by its big old volcano. This undersea vent started erupting, and over many centuries lava built land. Then the mountain cooled off and—*voilà*—you had an island. Same way Hawaii was built, same way Iceland was built. Happens all the time.

"Santorini was pretty big back then, I figure. There are still about thirty square miles of it left, sitting there in the bay on the site of the old volcano. I don't really know how big it might've been before 1450 B.C."

"Which is when the eruption occurred?"

"Right. The eruption. The Cataclysm. This kind of thing, too, happens all the time. A sleeping volcano starts rumbling to life, and then suddenly it pops. Sometimes you have a lot of advance warning—remember what happened when Mount Saint Helens started waking up in Washington? Everyone knew it was gonna blow. It was on the nightly news for a month.

"But then, other times, it's very sudden," Atwater continued. His voice dropped an octave. "There's a shake, a shudder, a shiver and then—*Kabloom!*

"We're pretty sure this is what happened with Santorini. The Minoan civilization that was there—a civilization that was tremendously advanced for its time—seemed to collapse almost overnight. So that's one indication. Why'd it disappear so suddenly, right? And then there's Plato's account. He said Atlantis was destroyed in one day and night. Vanished. Sank into the sea. So if you figure Santorini was Plato's 'Atlantis,' as most of us do, and then you put two and two together, you come up with the fact that Atlantis exploded and evaporated in a flash."

WE GAZED at the sea. It was a full-moon night now, and phosphorescence laced the breakers as they crashed upon the long beach, a beach visited, through the centuries, by Indians, pilgrims, pirates, philosophers—Henry David Thoreau himself—and, these days, by surf-and seashell-seekers from Boston and Plymouth and Providence, out upon the welcoming Cape for a much-needed weekend getaway.

"You know about Plato—Plato and Atlantis?"

> "THE STORY GOES THAT THE GOD TRITON GAVE THE ARGONAUTS A CLUMP OF EARTH WHICH THEY DROPPED INTO THE SEA, FORMING ATLANTIS."

"I do, somewhat."

"Good." His eyes gazed far out across the water. "And you want to learn more."

"Yes," I said. "All that you can teach me."

"Good," he said again. "I can show you some things. I can show you files. I can show you reports. I can show you photographs."

He waited for a reaction, but got none. I said eventually, "I've heard about these photographs of yours."

"Amos told you?" he asked.

"*You* told me. On the phone. You mentioned photographs."

"Ah," he said. "I'm getting careless. Gotta watch that. But, then, Amos did say that you could

> He promised to give me the pieces of the puzzle. "Then," he said, "you put 'em together."

be trusted. You *can* be trusted?"

"Are you sure they're not doctored?"

"No way. I've analyzed them at the Institute."

"Is that where they are?"

"No, they're here. They're right here in my briefcase. I took them. I pilfered them. I absconded with them. I stole 'em."

Although I had assumed this, I was nonetheless affected. "But why?" I asked.

"Because they were burying the whole Atlantis story, and because I think it's an important story that deserves to be told."

"This is fantastic, you know," I said. "It's simply unbelievable."

"It's believable. You'll see. I'll show you."

We turned, and walked slowly down from the dunes. The sound of the mighty ocean

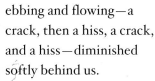

ebbing and flowing—a crack, then a hiss, a crack, and a hiss—diminished softly behind us.

"So Santorini, that's where Atlantis was," I said as we shook hands on the crushed-rock driveway of Beaver's property, having agreed to meet here again very early the next morning and get to work.

"You mean, where Atlantis *is*."

I smiled. "Okay, okay. Amos told me about this. The continued and continuing existence of Atlantis."

"It's true. Look—you know about all the many and varied theories of Atlantis's origin." It was as much a statement as a question.

"You mean how it might've been near Crete," I said, "but also might've been mid-Atlantic. In the Azores. Might've been in the Bahamas. Bimini perhaps." Atwater was clearly pleased that I had done at least some small bit of homework already, and that the basics of Atlantean history were things he would not have to tutor. "I know there are different theories," I continued, "different theories besides Crete and Santorini."

Atwater smiled, holding trump. "Well," he said, "in a way, all of the theories are true. All of 'em, not just Santorini."

"What?" I said, lost.

"Well, it was only one of them, when it was what it used to be. At first, long ago, it started in one

place—in Santorini, as we have agreed." He paused for effect, and then said, "But then Atlantis spread, ocean to ocean, colony to colony. It swam around the entire world. And today . . . today, Atlantis is everywhere."

The last thing Atwater said before we parted that night was, "Sleep tight."

PLATO ONCE wrote that Socrates once said, referring to Atlantis, "It has the very great advantage of being a fact and not a fiction." Atwater said the same. And Atwater, whatever his motivations—history? truth? vengeance?—said that he would help me to understand the elements of this great fact. He would point me in the right directions, give to me the accurate maps, explain to me the proper chronology of events, provide the names of the best-informed people. He would scatter before me the pieces of the puzzle. "Then," he said, "you put 'em together."

"I'll try," I told him. And this is a promise that I have earnestly sought to keep with this book.

"It'll be worth your while," Atwater said. "Because there's not just a good story here, there's a lesson in this." As he said that, he was staring intently at a strange, beguiling photograph, and his eyes moistened. "It's a riddle, a puzzle. It's a moral story.

"You know what it is?" he asked. "It's a test."

QUONDAM INSULA ATLANTIS

PLATO'S REPUBLIC

When Atlantis Was an Eden

"IN THE BEGINNING,"
Atwater told me, "there was the volcano.
Then there was the cooling of the
earth, then the building of an island.
It was a perfectly circular island with high mountains and deep valleys in its interior, and great cliffs at the shore. Meanwhile, elsewhere—somewhere not far away, somewhere in Africa—a species had come, first out of the depths of the ocean, thence to the lagoons, thence to the land, thence to the trees. This species was learning to walk. Upright. And in a geologic blink of the eye, this species set about conquering the world. And the best and brightest of this new species found its way to the circular island, and invented Atlantis." Then Atwater paused, smiled and said, "That's a rather brief synopsis, you understand."

way back, were connected to all other earthly primates, as the knee bone to the leg bone, the leg bone to the thigh bone. And these larger mammals were and are related to all Insectivora, all Marsupialia, all Rodentia. And these eventually were and are tied up with the reptiles, thence to other nonmammalian critters and fish, thence and thence and thence . . . all the way down to the ooze.

The ooze: primordial, fecund, slimy, wet. Home to water creatures, crawling forth.

*H*E TALKS like that sometimes: "in the beginning," "thence" and "whence" and "wherefore." He'll be ponderous—"Atlantis was doomed before it was doomed." And he'll be poetic—"Atlantis is as inscrutable as it is irrefutable." He takes himself seriously, then, realizing that he has done so, smiles sweetly and makes a small joke—in this case, "a rather brief synopsis."

Self-deprecation aside, he is saying, essentially, that Genesis is a rather brief synopsis of all things evolutionary, and that the keenest sons and daughters of Eden established their shiniest city in the hills of Atlantis. Atlantis was the jewel in the crown of the world, said Atwater. Atlantis ruled.

Or hoped to.

*"E*VOLUTIONARY science tells us that some species in any given age retain closer genetic ties to their ancestors than do other related species," says Peter Ward, professor of geologic science and zoology at the University of Washington at Seattle. "They fall less far from the tree, so to speak. These account for some of your 'missing links'—a subspecies with one foot in the old camp and one in the new, such as an almost-upright ape. These marooned species number among them certain . . . *anomalies*. Amphibians are obvious examples, being water creatures and land creatures both, and able

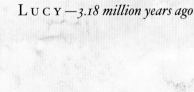

L U C Y —*3.18 million years ago*

*B*UT LET'S NOT skip ahead too quickly. Let's build a foundation.

While getting into no debates over creationism, let us agree that Darwin was a smart fellow and that the human inhabitants of the Edenic garden were but a few evolutionary steps from their Carnivora cousins. Whether God or nature—or both—led them along, there they were. Now then: the Carnivora were, in turn, a mere stone's throw from the simians who,

In 1981 the anthropologist Donald Johanson, finder of the oldest fossil bone of erect walking humans on record and author of Lucy, Beginnings of Humankind, *posed with the old girl's plaster-cast skull.*

16

to persevere in this schizophrenic condition over many generations, never casting their lot unequivocally with either their wet or dry condition. Bats are mammals that fly—an example of convergence, the notion that evolutionary opportunities provoke evolutionary responses."

Ward, a man of great sophistication who possesses an uncanny talent for making complexities comprehensible, is speaking by phone, without any understanding that our inquiry concerns Atlantis. Atwater suggested that I call Ward and have him lay some groundwork, and so I have. "It is widely—and mistakenly—assumed that species always progress, that they *improve over time*," continues Ward, whose landmark book, *Future Evolution*, sets all this out in greater detail. "Under this assumption, humans congratulate themselves on being the

> "EVOLUTION HAS ITS ANOMALIES. AMPHIBIANS ARE OBVIOUS EXAMPLES, BEING WATER AND LAND CREATURES BOTH, AND ABLE TO PERSEVERE IN THIS SCHIZOPHRENIC CONDITION."

last and best of evolutions—this conceit works in the same way that we used to believe that we were the last and best of God's labor. But the evolutionary record shows that species branch into available niches, and then adapt to them. When the niches change, species, like dinosaurs, become extinct. When niches stay stable, so do the species which occupy them. Sharks haven't changed appreciably in the last three hundred million years.

"When a large niche—for example, the one available for big-brained, bipedal primates with opposable thumbs—becomes available, it gets filled real fast. Humans went from the australopithecine named Lucy to Marie Curie in about a weekend, right? Swanscombe man to Steinheim man to Solo man to Rhodesian man to Neander-

TOWARD ATLANTEAN MAN

RADUS AD ATLANTEUM

SWANSCOMBE MAN
—*200,00-300,00 years ago*

STEINHEIM MAN —*200,000 years ago*

SOLO MAN —*125,000 years ago*

RHODESIAN MAN —*125,000 years ago*

NEANDERTHAL MAN —*110,000-30,000 years ago*

CRO-MAGNON MAN —*37,000-12,000 years ago*

ATLANTEAN MAN —*3,500 years ago-present*

The cave paintings at Lascaux, France, proved that man has been smarter longer.

thal man to Cro-Magnon man to modern man in about forty-eight hours—in geologic terms. An altogether astonishing achievement.

"Now, sometimes, even though evolution by natural selection is way too complicated to retrace its steps precisely, it still, on occasion, loops back on itself. Whales and dolphins are descended from land animals. Consider that point for a moment: Land animals became water animals. This seems contrary to our ideas of 'progress' and 'improvement,' but it is nonetheless true. Sometimes, if a 'progressive' animal meets a roadblock or changes its mind, then it pauses, or even 'retreats.' Wild horses, for instance, are not genetically different than farm horses, but they're in a state of what some would call regression because they've been forced into such a state. They find themselves alone, lost in the canyons, and it's adapt or die. They turn feral—or, rather, *return* to the feral."

Aha. I mention to Ward that his testimony reminds me of a

Homer, hallowed chronicler of advanced civilizations

story the Arctic adventurer Will Steger once told me. Steger had been trying to breed a hardier, feistier sled dog for an expedition to the North Pole. At his camp in Minnesota, Steger had introduced wolves among the huskies. Subsequently, there were several litters of cross-bred puppies. These were indeed rougher and tougher dogs, extremely well suited for hard work in the frozen north, and during several practice runs in Greenland and Iceland they performed admirably.

But, said Steger: "One night in northern Greenland, we were awoken by a dogfight. It was fierce, it was primal. I bolted from the tent, but there was nothing to be done. One dog was dead, and the other was just lying there, somewhat magisterially, having gone for the throat. I had no idea what had started it. Maybe this wolf-dog simply had too much wolf in her, and all of a sudden that part of her personality took over. All I knew was, I couldn't afford to be losing dogs on the trail. I stopped that breeding experiment pronto."

Ward's reaction: "Genetic memory. Wolfish instincts had been bred in the bones—*I am wolf, hear me howl*—and that night, the instincts clicked in. Why? Maybe some dream of wolf ancestors. Maybe because it was time to click. The wolf might have been hungry, and said, 'Hey, I'm a serious top-shelf carnivore. I can do this.' Reversion can be astonishingly quick sometimes.

"The thing I'd like to emphasize," Ward continues, "is that once the dog had gone back, she was all wolf again. She still had her training as a dog—she knew and remembered whatever she had been taught as a dog—but she was a wolf now.

Heinrich Schliemann was a real piece of work, and so were the palaces and other buildings he unearthed in the late 19th century—real pieces of work that proved Troy had truly existed and that there had been an ancient civilization at Mycenae.

A super wolf. A wolf with intellectual advantages, since she knew how the other half lived."

These basic scientific principles are detailed now, early on, as prelude. For as Atwater told me late one night: "It is important—*it is essential*—to comprehend the nature of evolution and devolution. These concepts must be distinctly understood from the very outset," he said softly, "or nothing wonderful can come of the story of Atlantis."

HUMANKIND, once it was up and running about two thousand millennia ago, went merrily on its world-beating ways. In the crucible of humanity, first in the Middle East and then all around the Mediterranean, several brown-, white- and red-skinned populations prospered, and some began to advance at remarkable rates. The extremely sophisticated cave paintings at Altamira, Lascaux and Chauvet are now dated as far back as 30,000 years ago. Clearly, there was civilized behavior long before Sumer, Harappa and other communities we hear so much of, long before Mycenae. The Greek city-states and the Roman Empire reached their respective zeniths in the few centuries before and after the birth of Christ, but we now know that there were advanced civilizations predating them.

Which brings us to Homer, hallowed chronicler of advanced civilizations.

For the longest time, it was thought that the great Greek epicist was more poet than historian,

MINOS RULED OVER THE CITY OF KNOSSOS AND THE ISLAND OF CRETE WITH AN IRON WILL AND AN IRON FIST. YOU DIDN'T WANT TO MEET HIS MINOTAUR.

more yarn spinner or even myth monger than truth teller. But Charles MacLaren didn't think so, and in his 1822 book, *A Dissertation on the Topography of the Plains of Troy*, MacLaren situated Priam's city in a section of what is now western Turkey. This land was characterized by fortress-like earthmounds that seemed, to MacLaren, straight out of *The Iliad*.

A devotee of MacLaren—and of Homer and Plato—was German businessman and archaeologist Heinrich Schliemann. Schliemann was a profoundly egomaniacal, self-promotional and acquisitive man, but whatever his flaws, Schliemann did find Troy. Following directions as sketched by MacLaren, he led an expedition in 1872 and 1873 that unearthed buildings and treasures dating, he thought, to the Trojan War.[1] Later study would reveal that Schliemann's plunder wasn't quite as old as that, but it also confirmed that, yes, indeed, Schliemann's plundered city had been Troy.

With its discovery, Troy and its battles were transformed, overnight, from myth to reality. And it became instantly clear that, nearly 3,200 years ago, there had existed sophisticated societies with sophisticated militaries. Most significantly for our purposes, as C. W. Ceram wrote in his 1951 study, *Gods, Graves and Scholars*, Schliemann "proved Homer's worth as historian."

---

[1] The treasures included the famous collection dubbed "Priam's gold." Among the most fabulous jewelry from the palace was an astonishing gold diadem that Schliemann melodramatically bestowed upon the brow of his Greek wife, Sophia, proclaiming her "my Helena."

Spyridon Marinatos, antiquities expert, Atlantis booster

Arthur John Evans discovered Minos's spectacular palace at Knossos (top).

$\mathcal{S}$CHLIEMANN, a believer in Knossos and Atlantis as well as Troy, did not dig in Crete after King Minos and the Minoans. But Arthur John Evans did.

The curator of the renowned Ashmolean Museum at Oxford University—later he became the regally titled "extraordinary professor of prehistoric archaeology"—Evans was already regarded as one of the world's eminent scavengers when in 1899 he first put spade to Cretan soil. The seal stones he came up with in short order pleased him; the structures he unearthed over time thrilled him and secured his fame.

"Sir Arthur found the city of Knossos, 'nuff said," Dr. Alfred S. McLaren asserts, leaning back in his chair in his dark, oiled-wood office at the Explorers Club in New York City. "On the hill of Kephela he found the palace that was built around 1900 B.C.; he found cities beneath the palace that take Knossos back another four hundred years. He found evidence of high artistic accomplishment and general sophistication. He found proof that Knossos was a cultural capital and that man was plenty smart as long as five thousand years ago."

McLaren, 33rd president of the august club, is a renowned finder of things himself—as commander of the submarine *Queenfish* during the cold war, he conducted the first survey of the Siberian continental shelf. He says, "I consider Sir Arthur Evans an explorer, and one of the very greatest of all discoverers. Even more than Schliemann did, he alchemized fiction as fact." Evans felt sure that this fantastic palace, with its hundreds of rooms laid out in an elaborate labyrinth, had once belonged to Minos, king of Crete. Much as Schliemann's find led to immediate reappraisals of Trojan and military history, Evans's discovery forced historians to reconsider the roots of all Western civilization. Were the Greeks really the first to have class and couth, or might there have been, centuries earlier, the Minoans (so named by Evans)? Crete "can fire the imagination of any archaeologist," wrote Spyridon Marinatos, Greece's director of antiquities, in 1972. "Here, indeed, was the birthplace of European civilization."

"Marinatos got it right, absolutely," says McLaren. "Just look at what was unearthed! A fourteen-hundred-room palace, two-story houses, a drainage system with terra-cotta pipes—bathtubs everywhere!—big clay jars showing evidence they'd been filled with wine, golden cups elaborately decorated. And the art! Those lovely ladies with painted lips, strong young men with curly hair. Looks to me like they had beauty parlors. The sublime dolphin frescoes. And for all that, no signs of weaponry, no fortification. Knossos was an earlier Athens or, if you will, an ancient Provincetown or SoHo—an artists' colony. But much, much larger. The Minoans really had something going there, way back when."

If Minos's nation did not have a land-based military, it did have a fleet, according to both ancient and modern historians. "The first person known to us by tradition as having established a navy is Minos," wrote Plato's contemporary Thucydides. And Richard Ellis, on the basis of harder evidence than was available to Thucydides, stated in his superb 1998 book, *Imagining Atlantis*, that "because it was totally unfortified—unusual in those battlesome days—Knossos required some means of defense, and nautical relics suggest that the city was protected by a massive fleet." The navy protected the isle of Crete and expanded Crete's reach, wrote Ellis: "The seafaring propensities of the Minoans also made it possible for them to colonize other islands, such as Strongyle [Santorini], seventy-five miles to the north."

Seventy-five miles of open sea is, today, nothing. Sailboats traverse the span on a lazy breeze, speedboats do it in a sprint. The telephone makes the citizens of Crete and Santorini neighbors. The citizens of Crete and Santorini share the precise same tastes in food, wine, politics, sports teams.

Back then, such a distance over water constituted a wall that had to be climbed with some considerable difficulty. This point is made only to emphasize: Crete and Santorini were discrete islands. There may have been shared cultural influences, shared traditions even. There may have been some intermarriage. But there was only one Crete. And there was only one, unique Santorini.

> "AND THE ART! ALL OF THAT ART! THE MINOANS REALLY HAD SOMETHING GOING THERE, WAY BACK WHEN."

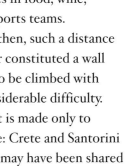

SANTORINI.

We arrive, now, at Atlantis. Our ship approaches the serene harbors of Santorini, and we have come home.

Look at Santorini not as it is now, beautiful though the resort may be. Look at it as it was then, when the island was whole, when The Cataclysm was a thing yet far off.[2] It is perfectly round and nestles in a protected part of the Aegean. Peloponnisos and its great capital, Sparta, are due west; Rhodes and, further on, Anatolia (Asia Minor) are due east; the large island of Cyclades and beyond it the upper Aegean Sea are to the north, and the large island of Crete and the greater Mediterranean Sea are to the south. Considering what we now know was happening in those places two thousand years before Christ, Santorini can be pictured as the hub of a great wheel of human achievement.

Ellis wrote that the Minoans colonized Santorini. Perhaps. Knossos might well have been dominant to the Santorin capital of Akrotiri, and King Minos might have been the region's top dog. Or it could have been the other way around: Akrotiri could have been Rome to Knossos's Corinth. There has long been debate: Did influence spread into Atlantis, building up a paradise, or out from Atlantis, as if from the mount? For the purposes of this examination, we need not worry about which eggs or chickens came first—Knossos or Akrotiri, Crete or Santorini, Minos or some Atlantean king. For whatever the case, "it is clear," Richard Ellis wrote, that "Akrotiri had been a town of some consequence. For its time, it was also immense, covering some thirty-one acres. There were two- and three-story buildings separated by narrow, winding streets; houses with substantial doors and stone staircases, with large windows to let in the sunlight." Ellis detailed how the larger buildings featured rooms built for specific functions, including bathrooms with bathtubs and gravity toilets. A sewer system of clay pipes ran beneath the streets.

This was *moderne*, no doubt about it, and there is little question that the settlement at Akrotiri was what Atlantis skeptics would call Minoan, or Minoan influenced. (From here forward, the terms "Minoan" and "Atlantean" should blur: we're talking about the same epoch and Aegean locale. Also, please retain Ellis's vision of Santorini—its touches from Martha Stewart, with wooden toilet seats and pottery covered with brilliantly colored flowers—for comparison with Plato's, shortly forthcoming.)

> DID INFLUENCE SPREAD INTO ATLANTIS, BUILDING UP A PARADISE, OR OUT FROM ATLANTIS, AS IF FROM THE MOUNT? WHICHEVER—ATLANTIS GREW, AND PROSPERED.

*F*RENCH VOLCANO expert Ferdinand Fouque was drawn to investigate the Santorin islands after an explosion there in 1866. The locals told Fouque that they had been scavenging antiqui-

---

[2] Keep in mind that the island that we call Santorini (or, alternately and less commonly, Santorin, Thera or Thíra) and which Plato knew as Strongyle was once much larger. The enormous catastrophe in roughly 1450 B.C. shattered it, leaving today's Santorini, Therasia, Nea Kameni, Pelea Kameni and Aspronisi. Santorini—so named in the Middle Ages for its patron saint, Irene—remains the largest of the five, and it is there that the city of Akrotiri is located.

POST VOLCANIC THERA

GREECE

AEGEAN SEA

TURKEY

Troy

Delphi
Thebes

Athens

Mycenae

CYCLADES

Sparta

Minoa

THERA
SANTORINI

RHODES

Knossos

CRETE

PLATO'S WORLD

TRUE OCEAN
ATLANTIS
EUROPE
ASIA
LIBYA
TRUE CONTINENT

THERASIA

VOLCANO

THERA

AKROTIRI

5 KM

ties—gold rings, other jewelry—for decades, inspiring the vulcanologist to turn archaeologist. Fouque unearthed bones, blades, tools, lamps and all manner of pottery and art. Analyzing his finds in an 1869 book, *A Prehistoric Pompeii*, Fouque wrote that the ancient, bygone men of Santorini "were laborers or fishermen; they cultivated cereals, made flour, extracted oil from olives, raised flocks of goats and sheep, fished with nets; they produced decorated vases and were acquainted with gold and probably copper."

Fouque concluded, based upon the depths of pumice, that the treasures he was unearthing had been buried after a massive volcanic eruption. He wrote that this immense blast had annihilated much of ancient Santorini, leaving only the outer-rim islands that we know today as Santorini and Therasia.

In 1883, the Indonesian volcanic island of Krakatau, west of Java in the Pacific Ocean, blew up in a fantastic way. The explosion, equivalent to 200 megatons of TNT, shot a dust cloud fifty miles high; the resulting tsunami killed nearly 40,000 people. Auguste Nicaise, a French scholar familiar with Fouque's work, took note, and gave a lecture in Paris entitled "The Vanished Lands: Atlantis, Thera, Krakatoa." His question: Could the

Plato founded his school, Academus, in a grove just beyond the Athens city limits. In that Eden he told his students of another: Atlantis.

Solon, forebear of Plato, was the one who first carried the history of Atlantis back to Athens. Egyptians gave it to him, and he handed it on.

stories of Thera, Krakatau and Atlantis be linked? The suggestion and its implications lay dormant until the mid–twentieth century when Spyridon Marinatos published *On the Legend of Atlantis*, in which he tied all of this up with Plato.

PLATO. Finally to Plato. Plato started it, of course—this concern with Atlantis. He gave the idea of Atlantis a name and he gave it a history. In the manner that Troy had its Homer and King Minos found his Boswell in Thucydides, Atlantis's chronicler for the ages was Plato.

Plato was the one who, in his dialogues *Timaeus* and *Critias*, written in the fourth century B.C., reported on a once-vast island "larger than Libya and Asia put together, with immense mountains, verdant valleys and fruit fair and wondrous and in infinite abundance." This magnificent Aegean Eden was crowned by a capital unlike any other, one of fabulous white-, black- and red-stone buildings laid out in five concentric circles, with a canal system running throughout to allow transport of produce from several ports which were "full of vessels and merchants coming from all parts who, from their numbers, kept up a multitudinous sound of human voices, and din and clatter." A busy, bustling heaven on earth. A place that sounds precisely like our Santorini, with its emerald city, Akrotiri.

Yes, okay, there are problems. To best understand them, we should dip further into Plato. What did he actually write of Atlantis?

He wrote of his ancestor, Solon, who encountered some Egyptians who told him of a huge island beyond "the strait which you [Athenians]

METROPOLIS ATLANTIS

call the Pillars of Hercules . . . On this island of Atlantis has risen a powerful and remarkable dynasty of kings, who ruled the whole island, and many other islands as well and parts of the continent."

Problems, problems: Santorini, even when whole, was nowhere near as big as Libya and Asia put together—especially when we realize that "Libya," to Plato, meant the whole of Africa less Egypt. Also, the "Pillars of Hercules" were, in fact, the Straits of Gibraltar, so anything beyond them from the direction of Athens was situated in the Atlantic Ocean, not the Aegean Sea. As far as Santorini-as-Atlantis is concerned, we have strike one on the *what*, strike two on the *where*. Strike three comes with the *when*: Plato wrote that the Egyptians told Solon of a people who had lived nine thousand years ago. Okay, now, without going into more cultural history or anthropology, let us concede this: there was no advanced civilization in the Mediterranean or Aegean—or anywhere—nine thousand years before Plato, never mind nine thousand years before Solon. And while there were indeed sophisticated societies up and running nine *hundred* years before Solon, and in fact many Atlantologists have argued that Plato exaggerated everything—size, time—by a factor of ten, to make sure that his listeners were paying attention, we're not going to argue this point. Rather than argue about this, we are, in fact, going to make final concessions: Atlantis was not in the Atlantic as Plato indicated, and Atlantis was not as big as

BEFORE ITS FALL, ATLANTIS WAS A PERFECT CIRCLE, IN EVERY MEANING OF THE WORD *CIRCLE*, AND IN EVERY MEANING OF THE WORD *PERFECT*.

either Africa or Asia, much less the size of both of them put together.

What we *are* going to argue, with help from people smarter than we are, is that the greatest of all philosophers was employing a tricky methodology that involved cloaking fact within metaphor.

To put it more simply: He was stretching a truth to get at a greater truth.

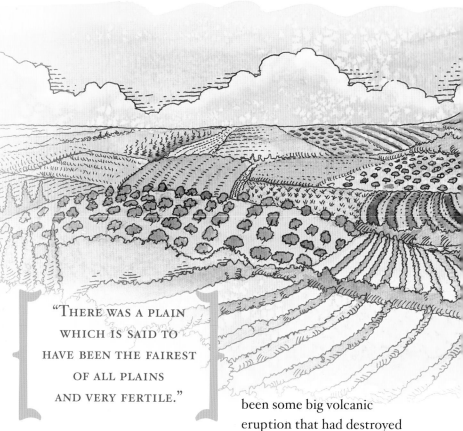

"PLATO was a teacher of moral and political philosophies, not history," says Chris Benfey, professor of literature at Mount Holyoke College in Massachusetts. "With the Atlantis story, he was trying to teach his fellow Greeks that something approaching perfection was possible in structuring a just, prosperous society. It had happened before, Plato said, and it can happen again. He was also teaching the perils of hubris, greed and aggression. It wasn't a history lesson—the history of Santorini was, frankly, of little consequence to Plato. His was a civics lesson. Plato as much as told his students that he was exaggerating to prove his point when

> "THERE WAS A PLAIN WHICH IS SAID TO HAVE BEEN THE FAIREST OF ALL PLAINS AND VERY FERTILE."

he had Crito say, 'Listen, Socrates, to a tale which, though strange, is certainly true, having been attested by Solon, who was the wisest of the seven sages.' Strange but true: it sounds like *Ripley's Believe It or Not*.

"Plato was no fool; he knew what he was doing. He certainly knew about Santorini, Crete and King Minos—Thucydides had written about them only a few years earlier. He knew the reputation of the Minoan civilization as an exemplary thing. He knew of the seafaring ways of the Minoans and their colonizations of other islands in the Aegean and Mediterranean. He knew that there had

Plato, a former slave, told his students that man could be cruel or kind, and that there were consequences.

been some big volcanic eruption that had destroyed some big island—probably Santorini—somewhere in some ocean—probably the Aegean. And he knew, furthermore, that the great, sophisticated Minoan civilization had disappeared almost overnight. He did not know why. No one did, and no one does today, not for sure. But he accurately detailed a collapsing culture and a cataclysm—*The* Cataclysm, if you like. He had all the ingredients of an excellent fable with a bunch of nifty moral messages at the end: thou shalt not kill, thou shalt not covet thy neighbor's goods, thou shalt not get too big for thy britches. It was irresistible.

"If he had told his students, 'Gather round, I want to tell you of Santorini,' they would have said, 'Been there, heard that.' They would have had their own ideas on the matter, ideas about corrupt politicians, an overextended navy, whatever. You know how college kids are—they all think they know more than the teacher. They would have tuned out poor old Plato.

"But by giving Santorini a new name and moving it to a bigger ocean, thereby allowing it to be a bigger and more brilliant place—and a place

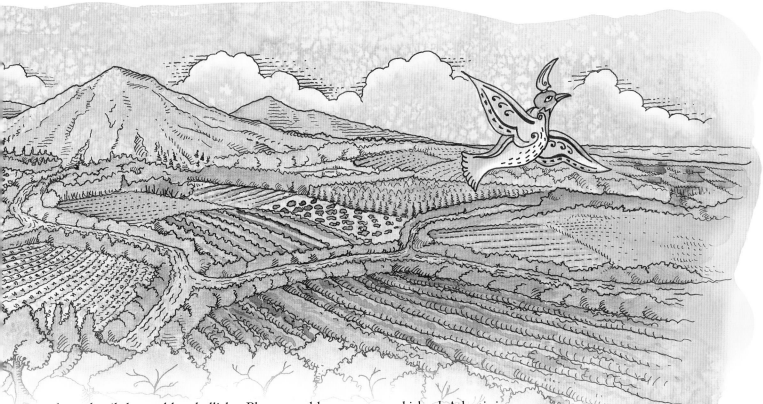

whose details he could embellish—Plato was able to develop larger themes and keep his audience riveted. Just as a quick for-instance: Part of his story, near the climax, tells of a war between Athens and Atlantis, and Plato's noble Athens repels the rapacious Atlanteans. Now, Greece might well have been able to fend off an invading force from little Santorini. Where's the heroism in that? But by beating back the navy of a country bigger than Africa and Asia—well, that's something to brag about, and that's the sign of a great nation, a nation favored by the gods. Since Plato was busily constructing the philosophical underpinnings of his city and country—making Greece great and making Greece *believe* it was great—this was one way of saying that right makes might, and if we continue down the path as I, Plato, am paving it, then we'll all be okay. More than okay; we'll be blessed.

"Was there, in fact, a war between Santorini and Athens? Probably. Why not? What about the other details in Plato's story? Pretty accurate, I'd say. Just think about it: Santorini's a perfectly

Chris Benfey, professor of literature at Mount Holyoke College

round island, Atlantis is a perfectly round continent, with a perfectly round city at its center. High art and intellect of a supreme order on Santorini, ditto for Atlantis. Colonizing instincts, ditto for Atlantis. Big *ka-boom*, big *ka-boom*. A lost island, a lost continent.

"Plato's descriptions should not be taken as journalistic. They should, however, be taken as pretty much the way they were—writ very, very large."

❧

THIS, THEN, was what Santorini looked like on its best day. This, said Plato, was Atlantis:

"Toward the sea and halfway down the length of the whole island, there was a plain which is said to have been the fairest of all plains and very fertile. Near the plain again, and also in the center of the island at a distance of about fifty stadia, there was a mountain not very high on any side." The Atlanteans living there were rich, said Plato, beyond any previous

wealth of kings and potentates—they enjoyed an affluence "not likely ever to be again, and they were furnished with everything that they needed, both in the city and in the country."

Atlantis, dominant, imported goods from wherever it chose, even though "the island itself provided most of what was required by them for the uses of life. In the first place, they dug out of the earth whatever was to be found there, solid as well as fusile, and that which is now only a name and was then something more than a name, oricalcum, was dug out of the earth in many parts of the island, being more precious in those days than anything except gold. There was an abundance of wood for carpenters' work, and sufficient maintenance for tame and wild animals. Moreover, there was a great number of elephants in the island; for as there was provision for all sorts of animals, both of those which live in lakes and marshes and rivers, and also for those which live in mountains and on plains, so there was for the animal which is the largest and most voracious of all."[3]

Plato's Atlantis had an immense agrarian industry which produced everything from fruits and vegetables to fabulous essences distilled from rare flowers. "With such blessings the earth freely furnished them; meanwhile they went on constructing their temples and palaces and harbors and docks." The infrastructure of the capital was fantastic; having been built when it was, it makes construction of the Brooklyn Bridge appear a trifle. From the sea, Atlanteans dug a canal

of three hundred feet in width, one hundred feet in depth and fifty stadia in length, leading to an interior harbor "and leaving an opening sufficient to enable the largest vessels to find ingress." The royal palace was built on a partially man-made inner island; rock and soil were quarried to create landfill. The circular city was enclosed. "The entire circuit of the wall, which went round the outermost zone, they covered with a coating of brass, and the circuit of the next wall they coated with tin, and the third, which encompassed the citadel, flashed with the red light of oricalcum."

The metropolis enjoyed the most sophisticated landscaping and architecture; there were glorious fountains and many public baths—separate structures for royalty, men, women, horses and cattle. In the grove of Poseidon grew "all manner of trees of wonderful height and beauty, owing to the excellence of the soil." There were "many temples built and dedicated to many gods; also gardens and places of exercise, some for men, and others for

---

[3]Do not put elephants, indigenous only to Africa and India today, in the column of items that might disprove Atlantis. The islands of the Dodecanese and Peloponnese, including Santorini and Crete, were connected to the African mainland as recently as Lower Pleistocene times.

horses in both of the two islands formed by the zones; and in the center of the larger of the two there was set apart a racecourse of a stadium in width, and in length allowed to extend all round the island, for horses to race in.[4]

"The interior featured a level plain, itself surrounded by mountains which descended towards the sea; it was smooth and even, and of an oblong shape. The surrounding mountains were celebrated for their number and size and beauty, far beyond any which still exist, having in them also many wealthy villages of country folk, and rivers, and lakes, and meadows supplying food enough for every animal, wild or tame, and much wood of various sorts, abundant for each and every kind of

work. A huge ditch brought water to the plain from the mountains, and canals extended into the verdant valleys."

These canals were at intervals of a hundred stadia, and via these canals the Atlanteans brought down the wood from the mountains to the city, and conveyed "the fruits of the earth in ships, cutting transverse passages from one canal into another, and to the city. Twice in the year they gathered the fruits of the earth—in winter having the benefit of the rains of heaven, and in the summer the water which the land supplied, when they introduced streams from the canals.

"As to the population . . ."

INDEED, as to the population: we will deal with the population—or, rather, the *de*population—in the next part of this book.

"What was The Cataclysm like?" Atwater asked as he looked out upon the Atlantic one chilly October evening. "Must have been awesome, certainly. But that's another of those what-when-where questions that don't interest me an awful lot.

"What I'd like to know: I'd like to know the *why* of The Cataclysm."

He turned, and looked at his shoes a long moment before starting for the cabin. "I don't think I ever will know the why of it," he said softly. "Not for sure." He limped down the path in that slow, stiff-legged walk of his.

---

[4] The gymnasiums ("places of exercise") are believed to have been the first anywhere on the planet. Also, whether societies earlier than Atlantis staged contests involving their animals is uncertain. It is unknown whether Atlanteans wagered on their horse races. Perhaps in their virtuous era they did not, and then, later, debased, they did.

UBIQUE NAUFRAGIUM EST

CRIMES AND PUNISHMENT
The Sinking of Atlantis

ATWATER TOLD ME ONE NIGHT:
"There have been many other cataclysms.
Really cataclysmic cataclysms. When
Krakatau blew, half the earth shook.
When Tambora blew, a cubic mile of mountain
was shot straight into the air. When the earthquake hit Lisbon, sixty thousand people died. In
1896 the Sanriku tsunami—a wall of water you
couldn't see the top of—slammed into Japan at
nearly five hundred miles an hour. Now, when
you think about Japan, don't just think about
the earthquakes and the tidal waves. Think
about Hiroshima. Nagasaki. And when you think
about earthquakes, think of San Francisco times
ten. Pinatubo times ten." Then Atwater paused, and
said: "I think about all of this all the time. And still, I
don't think there's ever been anything to compare with
the sinking of Atlantis."

TO SET UP the Atlantean mystery, let us look at the Minoan mystery. "All we know about the end of the Minoan civilization," Richard Ellis wrote succinctly in his book on Atlantis, "is that it occurred suddenly."

What happened? Spyridon Marinatos was the first to suggest, in 1939, that Crete had been wracked by tsunamis and earthquakes associated with the huge explosion at Santorini, an eruption that, by the mid–twentieth century, had been accurately placed circa 1450 B.C. (a crisp nine hundred years before Plato, much to the aid and comfort of Atlantologists holding out for the factor-of-ten theory). Another idea about the precipitous decline and fall of the Minoan empire posits a conquest by the Mycenaeans of Greece, whose cause may have been abetted by earthquake-spurred tsunamis that subsequently swamped the Minoan fleet.

Virtually all theories about the extinction of Minoan culture involve a big bang on Santorini. Bearing this in mind, there are additional points to be made. First, an explosion ties in with the history of Atlantis, as we know it from Plato. Second, this big-bang thesis bolsters the case that the center of Minoan culture—the capital, the ideal city, the true Atlantis—was on Santorini, not Crete. Knossos, after all, did survive The Cataclysm, albeit in a tattered state. If Knossos had been the hub—if Crete and not Santorini had been Plato's Atlantis—then Minoan civilization might have been able to pick itself up, dust itself off and get back into the race. As it was, Santorini disappeared at the same time that the Minoans (and Atlanteans) seemed to lose their reason for being.

Ipso facto, i.e. and ergo.

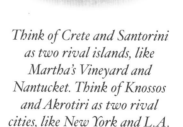

Think of Crete and Santorini as two rival islands, like Martha's Vineyard and Nantucket. Think of Knossos and Akrotiri as two rival cities, like New York and L.A.

WHETHER OR NOT Crete and Santorini were ever the pacifist paradises that have been painted by some scholars, they had certainly developed expansionist tendencies by the time they were sacked by fate. We have talked already about the Minoan navy as an offensive as well as defensive unit. The powerful cities of Knossos and Akrotiri were on the move, perhaps ill advisedly. Overextension of dominion wasn't new even in 1500 B.C.; it is, as we know, always dangerous.

Reaching too far humbled Rome and London, Napoleon and Hitler. It is tempting to conclude that somehow, some way, the Minoans came a cropper through their own aggression, were brought down by their own hand. However . . .

"There's no evidence of that," says Mount Holyoke College's Professor Benfey. "We have evidence of their colonizing, but no evidence that this colonization led to their downfall. We have no evidence of any advance and subsequent retreat comparable to Rome's retreat from Britain, or Britain's retreat from America and Australia and China and India and South Africa and all the other places Britain retreated from. All that we see with the Minoans is that they were there, all over the Mediterranean, and then—*poof!*—they vanished."

This is not altogether true—the *poof* part isn't—as we will shortly see. There's solid evidence of a Minoan diaspora, a dispersal of Minoan influence throughout the civilized world. This indicates that there were indeed survivors of whatever holocaust beset the society. You, my dear readers, might know a Minoan today, and so might I. "I've got Minoan blood," Atwater told me late one night, "or something quite like it." He waited for my reaction for a good long moment, and then he smiled, thereby defusing the moment.

ONE THEORY regarding the Minoan dooms-day affords the opportunity to introduce a very interesting character in the modern Atlantean drama. James W. Mavor Jr., for years a colleague of Atwater's at Woods Hole, wondered if a comet might have bludgeoned Santorini.

Mavor, born in 1923, joined Woods Hole in the postwar years and established himself as a talented, energetic oceanographic engineer. One of the designers of the famous deep-water submersible Alvin, he first became interested in Atlantis in the 1960s after reading the landmark paper by Angelos Galanopoulos, *Tsunamis Observed on the Coast of Greece from Antiquity to the Present Time*, in which the author, a lecturer on seismology at Athens University, hypothesized that Atlantis's disappearance should be credited to the Santorini eruption.[5]
In 1966 Mavor went to the Aegean, already convinced, as he later put it, "that Atlantis did actually, physically exist, not in the Atlantic Ocean, on the grand scale of legend, or in the North Sea, the Bahamas, the East Indies, South America, Spain, the Indian Ocean or other parts of the world which have been mentioned as its location, but in a lesser, more familiar dimen-

> WHEN THE VOLCANO ON
> SANTORINI BLEW, THE EARTH
> SHIVERED, THE EARTH SHOOK.
> THEN THE EARTH OPENED WIDE.
> THE SEA ENGULFED.

[5] Galanopoulos saw the explosion's impact far and wide. Noting the temporal coincidence of the eruption and other famous historical events, he said that the massive blast on Santorini could well have been responsible not only for the destruction of Atlantis, but for the Phaethon story of a stopping sun (volcanic ash would have shielded it from view), the biblical plagues of Egypt (climate change due to the ash would have spurred them) and even the parting of the Red Sea (the emptying and refilling was caused by tsunamis). Moses meets Atlantis.

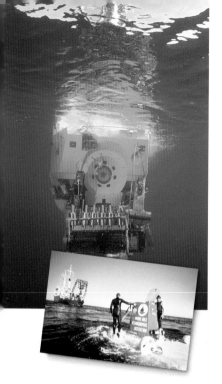

When Alvin (top) ascended, it brought up news that was worthy of Page One.

sion, in a sea utterly familiar to Plato." Mavor headed straight for Santorini.

Mavor's discoveries there, coming as they did from an eminent American scientist affiliated with the country's preeminent oceanographic institution, created a large stir. News coverage of Mavor's expedition, the Helleno-American Multi-Disciplinary Scientific Investigation of Thera and Quest for Lost Atlantis, was positively lathered. MOAT BELIEVED TO BE PART OF ATLANTIS IS FOUND IN AEGEAN SEA read one headline; A MINOAN CITY, FOUND AFTER 3,400 YEARS, IS LINKED TO ATLANTIS, blared another. Mavor was not reticent. In a book about his expeditions, *Voyage to Atlantis*, he wrote not only that "Thera was a strategic center of maritime commerce and a cult center, as Plato said of the metropolis of Atlantis," but also, more boldly, "Perhaps the most startling discovery I made was not Atlantis itself, but the realization that Atlantis had lain exposed for centuries, for all to see, if they but knew what to look for."[6]

For years after his Santorin expeditions, Mavor shared Galan-opoulos's conviction that a volcanic eruption on Santorini did in Atlantis. But his thinking even-

tually changed. In the 1980s, a war raged between scientists at the University of California at Berkeley, led by Dr. Luis Alvarez, and professors at Dartmouth, led by Charles Drake and Charles Officer, over what had caused the dinosaur extinctions 65 million years ago. Berkeley argued that a huge comet had smashed into the earth, raising a massive cloud of debris which, over time, cooled the planet and frosted the big beasts. Dartmouth, meanwhile, maintained that the extinctions were due to massive volcanic activity, which threw up the black ceiling that chilled the earth. Berkeley, with the sexier theory, gained adherents even as Dartmouth shouted, "Where's your crater?" It all got very unpleasant.

Mavor, like many, was quite taken with the Alvarez research. "The comet theory of destruction, which has been around for at least two centuries, has gained sudden credibility," he wrote in 1987 in *Oceanus*, a magazine published by Woods Hole. Mavor argued that such catastrophism "seeks to explain boundaries and other discontinuities in the cultural, biological or geological record left in the soils and rocks of the earth's crust." Mavor then cited as one such cultural and geological discontinuity "the eruption and collapse of Thera."

As we see, Mavor did not in fact *say* that a comet sank Atlantis. What Mavor did claim was that a host of disasters

---

[6]"Covering Mavor has always been fun," says David Perry (left), a longtime reporter for the *Lowell Sun* in Massachusetts. "He always put himself on the line. I'll never forget the press conference in Boston way back when. It was wild. And then he did it again with the comet theory—the bit about how a comet whacked Atlantis. Wild! But up here, Woods Hole is like the Red Sox, it's like beans and cod and Kennedys. It's sacrosanct, and so Mavor's an absolute god. When he said that an asteroid had nuked Atlantis, everyone around here said, 'Well, there you have it—I guess it was an asteroid that nuked Atlantis!'"

occurring in the millennia before Christ's birth—not only the sinking of Santorini but also the plagues of Egypt, the Greek deluge of Deukalion in Greece and even Noah's flood—may—*may*—"refer to a series of devastating astronomical events."

Qualifiers notwithstanding, all of a sudden everyone was talking about asteroids bludgeoning Atlantis.

Charles Officer was not. Or, rather, he was talking about the subject, but not kindly.

"Look," he says a decade later, during an interview at Dartmouth, "I don't want to quarrel with a fellow New Englander, but volcanoes did in the dinosaurs, and a volcano did in Atlantis. In my book, *The Great Dinosaur Extinction Controversy*, I deal with this: catastrophism almost always has a more certain answer in volcanic activity than in some speculative comet. Yes, comets have hit the earth in times gone by. But, as with the dinosaurs, where's the evidence of Atlantis's comet? We *know* it had a volcano. Read Galanopoulos. He's got it right."

Following Officer's instructions, in Angelos Galanopoulos's *Atlantis: The Truth Behind the Legend* we find, "Finally we have shown that volcanic activity on a really stupendous scale did take place in the Eastern Mediterranean in the middle of the Bronze Age, that this activity was centered on the island of Santorin, and that it resulted in, among other things, the sudden disappearance of the whole center of an inhabited, small, round island. The case, therefore, for the identification of Santorin with the ancient Metropolis of Atlantis is extremely strong, and is supported by a considerable amount of corroborative evidence of very great interest."

These words are contained in a chapter which Galanopoulos boldly, emphatically, almost arrogantly entitled, "Case Proven."

Charles Officer, defender of volcano theory, no friend of comets

"I HATE TO GO against a buddy," Atwater said early one morning over coffee, "but I've always sided with the volcano folks. I liked Mavor. An extremely bright, hardworking guy—always. We agreed on a lot of things—the Red Sox, the Patriots, most of the stuff about Atlantis. But concerning the volcano-versus-comet thing, well, we never saw eye to eye on that one."

Atwater was asked if the esteemed Mavor was involved in The Atlantis Project—the secret operation that is, presumably, still ongoing at Woods Hole, and that Atwater was slowly unveiling for me.

"That," said Atwater, "is a question I will not answer."

GALANOPOULOS wrote of "volcanic activity on a really stupendous scale." What is a really stupendous scale?

Let's start by considering that mild volcanic action can impact weather half a world away—volcanoes, in other words, always have aftershocks. As David Ewing Duncan, the noted vulcanologist based in quake-prone San Francisco, tells us during an interview at a bayside café in Sausalito, "A volcano's impact is seldom slight. A volcano can shift ground a hundred miles off, can create a tsunami a thousand feet high, can destroy an island or create an island—all of the Hawaiian islands were formed by a volcanic vent beneath the ocean, as was Iceland, as were those three smaller islands in the Santorini cauldron, all of which have surfaced in the centuries since the Atlantis Cataclysm.

The aftershocks of the 1991 explosion at Pinatubo were felt around the world for a year, and are still being felt locally today. Said one villager a week after the blast: "This is what Atlantis went through, I am sure."

"For a look at how a volcano affects everything, take Pinatubo, the five-thousand-footer that blew in the Philippines in 1991. In the years since, each and every rainstorm in the area has brought torrents of hot volcanic mud rushing down to the plains below. More than a hundred villages have been buried, and the flows may continue for another decade. Furthermore, Pinatubo exported the misery. Its mushroom cloud of debris floated on the winds and changed climate everywhere. It wrecked the 1992 summer season on the New Jersey shore.

"And Pinatubo wasn't a biggie, not in any historic sense."

I WENT to Atwater who had been studying vulcanism ever since he became enmeshed in the Atlantis story. I asked for a synopsis of global volcanic history, so I could place The Cataclysm at Santorini in some sort of context. He was direct, as usual, if drier than normal; it was as if he were cloaking the horror in facts, in bloodless statistics.

"We have earthquakes and volcanoes to look at," he said. "Earthquakes first. The 1960 quake in Chile measured nine point five on

We always remember the spectacle—the mountain or the quake—but too seldom the victims, such as those in the shadow of Pinatubo (above) and in Chile (left).

the Richter scale—the most powerful ever—and tsunamis caused by it killed scores of people on the Big Island of Hawaii, five thousand miles away. The Great Lisbon Earthquake of 1775 saw the ocean rush in and kill sixty thousand. That was nothing in terms of fatalities compared with China's quake in 1556, when nearly a million died, or the 1737 quake in Calcutta that claimed three hundred thousand, or the 1923 quake that demolished Tokyo. In terms of deaths, San Francisco in 1906 was light, but it did measure a heavy eight point three on the Richter scale."

"Clark Gable did a great job of saving people," I offered.

"Yes, well," Atwater said without a smile. "Among terrible volcanoes, we have Papandayang in Java blowing in 1772, Skaptar blowing in Iceland in 1783 and Mount Pelee blowing on Montserrat just recently, in 1997. Two big ones you've certainly heard of were Tambora, which blew on Sumbawa in 1815, and Krakatau, which also blew in the Pacific, also in Indonesia, in 1883. This was the same kind of volcano as Santorini's, and it caused—"

"I saw that movie too," I interrupted. "The one about Krakatau." Again, Atwater didn't smile. In fact, he glowered.

"Look," he finally said. "This is not a joke. Atlantis is not a joke. Cataclysm is not a joke. It was a terrible, terrible thing that happened on Santorini. A volcano as large as that occurs once in a millennium. It is horrific. It is . . ."

He stopped. He took off his eyeglasses and put them on the table. "I've got a friend," he said, "who has written about this. He's smart, he's good. I don't usually take to Harvard guys, but I like George. I'd like you to have a brief talk with him before we continue. He lives out here on the Cape, and I think the two of you should sit down together and have a cup of coffee."

AND SO IT WAS that, on a Saturday morning in early winter, George Howe Colt and I sat for breakfast at Marie's, a diner in Pocasset.

Colt, a slim, curly-haired fellow, was exceedingly pleasant. He was less rigorously serious than Atwater, but approached his topic in a no-nonsense way. The topic was, essentially, chaos: why humankind is romantically drawn to the notion of it, how we react to it. Colt is the author of *The Enigma of Suicide* and *The Strange Allure of Disasters: Why We Can't Look Away.* It was this second, quite extraordinary work that Atwater had me read before I sat with Colt.

Atwater introduced us, got his coffee and quickly slipped out the door—furtively, I thought. Colt and I exchanged pleasantries, talked about the stunningly beautiful autumn that Cape Cod had enjoyed, talked about last weekend's Patriots game and the team's prospects the next day, talked about nothing at all. Then the clam fritters came, and I started the tape recorder. Colt's salient testimony follows:

"Why are we so fascinated by disaster? Part of it is sheer mind-bending spectacle. I was talking to a television exec for my study, and you know what he told me? Talking about that asteroid movie on TV, he said, 'A huge rock, exploding buildings, people fleeing . . . what's not to love?' Can you believe he said that?

"Now, in an actual disaster, as

Earthquakes such as San Francisco's (above) and Tokyo's (below) are, quite often, not isolated events. Hawaii has had volcano-linked quakes, as has Iceland. As did Atlantis.

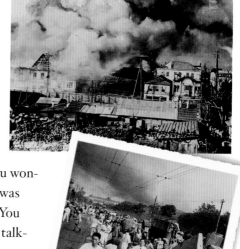

opposed to a movie, real people die. But while our interest in looking may make us feel guilty, we can't take our eyes off the real thing, either. As the Roman poet Lucretius put it, 'It is pleasant, when the sea runs high, to view from land the distress of another.' You wonder if old Lucretius was looking at Atlantis. You wonder if he'd been talking to Plato.

"Disasters evoke the mix of horror and voyeurism that makes us rubberneck while driving past an accident—but on a colossal scale. All of life's great themes are compressed into a few moments. Disasters can be disconcertingly comforting: they remind us of life's

George Howe Colt, disaster theorist, compassionate man

*"Women and children
heaped up mountain high
Limbs crushed under which
ponderous marble lie.
Say what advantage
can result to all
From wretched Lisbon's
lamentable fall?"*
—VOLTAIRE

preciousness. We are still alive. Someone else is dead, but we are still alive. Disasters make us think about blessings.

"Another thing, especially pertinent to Atlantis: fictionalizing disasters is one way to sanitize them, and mythologizing them is another. The more we layer a disaster with metaphor, the easier it is to ignore the burned flesh, the screams in the water. When we look at a gold watch salvaged from the *Titanic*, do we see an object that once sat in the pocket of a human being who died a premature or tragic death or, rather, do we see the end of an era, the death of chivalry, the hubris of *Homo sapiens*? When we look at the dolphin frescoes of Knossos, do we glimpse a community of flesh-and-blood Minoan artisans at work, or their hard-to-know Atlantean cousins across the bay in Santorini, people we safely cannot touch because their relics

Earthquake at Lisbon. Vol. 2, p. 86.

were shattered beyond finding?

"Even the vocabulary of disaster gets cleansed of blood. No one in Pompeii suffocated—they were 'encased in tombs of ash.' No one on the *Titanic* drowned—they 'went to their watery graves.' Atlantis didn't suffer and burn as if hit by a thousand bombs—it 'slipped beneath the waves.' Eventually, tragedy is obliterated by such linguistic stunts.

"Real stunts, too. I was just reading about a company in the Virgin Islands that salvaged a propeller from the *Lusitania* and melted it down into souvenir golf clubs. Tragedy vanishes when things like that happen. Always remember: what happened to Atlantis was a terrible, terrible event.

"We should remember what Voltaire said about these . . . again, I'll call them stunts. He thought this kind of reductionism was cruel. That's his word, not mine—'cruel.' He had been upset by a more than usually pompous essay by Alexander Pope, who, writing about the Lisbon earthquake, argued that all disasters were, like all things, the work of God, and therefore for the universal good.

'One truth is clear,' Pope wrote, 'whatever is, is right.' Voltaire was incensed by this. He shot back with graphic descriptions of Lisbon's suffering. I can quote them by heart: 'Women and children heaped up mountain high/Limbs crushed under which ponderous marble lie.' He concluded by asking, 'Say what advantage can result to all/From wretched Lisbon's lamentable fall?'

"Or, you could fairly well ask, in a paraphrase: wretched Atlantis's lamentable fall."

CHASTENED, I returned to my inquiries. Before learning more about the Atlantean Cataclysm, I now felt that I needed to know more about the Atlantean people—the flesh-and-blood people. I returned to Plato, and picked up in the *Critias* with "As to the population . . . there were many special laws affecting the several kings inscribed about the temples; but the most important was the following: They were not to take up arms against one another . . . For many generations, as long as the divine nature lasted in them, they were obedient to the laws, and well affectioned towards the gods, whose seed they were; for they possessed true and in every way great spirits, uniting gentleness with wisdom in the various chances of life, and in their intercourse with one another. They despised everything but virtue, caring little for their present state of life, and thinking lightly of the possession of gold and other property, which seemed only a burden to them; neither were they intoxicated by luxury; nor did wealth deprive them of their self-control;

"THEY THEN, BEING UNABLE TO BEAR THEIR FORTUNE, BEHAVED UNSEEMLY, AND TO HIM WHO HAD AN EYE TO SEE GREW VISIBLY DEBASED . . ."

but they were sober, and saw clearly that all these goods are increased by virtue and friendship with one another."

Then, a turn: "When the divine portion began to fade slowly, and became diluted too often and too much with the mortal admixture, and the human nature got the upper hand, they then, being unable to bear their fortune, behaved unseemly, and to him who had an eye to see grew visibly debased, for they were losing the fairest of their precious gifts; but to those who had no eye to see the true happiness, they appeared glorious and blessed at the very time when they were becoming tainted with unrighteous ambition and power. Zeus, the god of gods, who rules according to law, and is able to see into such things, perceiving that an honorable race was in a woeful plight, and wanting to inflict punishment on them that they might be chastened and improve, collected all the gods into their most holy habitation, which, being placed in the center of the world, beholds all created

of extraordinary violence, and in a single dreadful day and night . . . the island of Atlantis was swallowed up by the sea and vanished."

Perspective: The bomb was very little compared to what happened, when cameras were not at hand, on the Indonesian isles of Tambora and Krakatau. And on Atlantis.

things. And when he had called them together, he spoke as follows."

And at this point, as Plato scholars know, the unfinished *Critias* dialogue breaks off, as if our eavesdropping on a congress of the gods debating the fate of Atlantis is something that simply mustn't be done.

Elsewhere in Plato's *Dialogues*, in the *Timaeus*, we do learn what happened, if only in digest form: "At a later time there were earthquakes and floods

We MUST confront that dreadful day and night.

The big blast at Santorini—the 1450 B.C. blast—has been estimated at 7,500 megatons, a figure arrived at by measuring ash and other evidence on the remnant islands.[7] It was, it is guessed, the second greatest eruption in mankind's history, after Tambora.

Tambora: Everyone had presumed that verdant Mount Tambora on the Indonesian island of Sumbawa was extinct, until, in early April 1815, the 13,000-foot mountain began to shake. In the largest eruption since the end of the last Ice Age, the island exploded with a force of between 20,000 and 25,000 megatons. Nine hundred miles away, a sea captain thought that he heard cannon fire and readied his ship, anticipating an imminent attack by pirates. More than 170 billion tons of volcanic debris was shot into the atmosphere; as far as 300 miles away, darkness reigned for three days. Ten thousand Sumbawans were killed instantly; eighty thousand more Indonesians died as a consequence of the resultant famine and disease. The cloud of ash roamed, affecting everything on the planet—to a much greater degree than Pinatubo's cloud did in our time. Eighteen-sixteen was the year without a summer on our earth; a killing frost ruined farms in Connecticut in August.

Santorini's explosion, if not quite as big as Tambora's, was bigger than Krakatau's. The classicist J. V. Luce employed this latter Indonesian eruption, which reduced an island to one third its former size in 1883, as a model for what happened to Atlantis. From Luce's *Lost Atlantis: New Light on an Old Legend*: "Vulcanologists agree that Krakatoa

---

7 A megaton equals a million tons. By contrast, the atom bomb at Hiroshima had a megatonnage of 0.02.

[Luce used the old spelling] is a volcano of the same type as Thera [Luce used Santorini's other name]. The two volcanoes have demonstrably been behaving in a similar way for as far back as we can trace their activity." Luce went on at great technical length to prove that the volcanoes on Krakatau and

Santorini were brethren, and then wrote of the well-documented Indonesian incident: "The sound of the explosion was heard over an enormous area. Blast waves broke windows and cracked walls up to 160 kilometers off. The explosion was heard in Madagascar, 3,000 miles away; it has been termed the loudest sound in recorded history. Aerial vibrations from the 10 A.M. explosion were detected all over the globe. . . . In recorded eruptions Krakatoa has no rival in the extreme violence of its culminating paroxysms, and in the catastrophic air- and sea-waves to which it gave rise."

Giant tsunamis went out in all directions, killing thousands. Nine hours after the eruption, a wave traveling at four hundred miles an hour slammed into the harbor at Calcutta. The destruction was enormous, as Luce detailed: "Nearly 300 towns and villages bordering the Sunda Strait were devastated, and 36,380 people lost their lives. The extent of the flooded areas was immense. The town of Tyringen, 48 kilometers from Krakatoa, was the first to suffer. Many houses near the sea were destroyed in a wave which swept in between 6 and 7 P.M. on 26 August. The same wave damaged Telok Betong in Sumatra, 72 kilometers away from the volcano. At 1 A.M. on 27 August, the

> WAS IT LIKE THAT: WAVES GOING OUT IN ALL DIRECTIONS, CRACKS IN THE EARTH APPEARING EVERYWHERE, THOUSANDS SCURRYING FOR SHELTER WHERE THERE WOULD BE NO SHELTER?

village of Sirik was submerged . . . Owing to the darkness and terror, reliable observation of the height of the waves was almost impossible."

Hiroshima, on the morning after, one straggling survivor, could stand in for Atlantis . . .

WHAT CAN we conjure of The Cataclysm at Atlantis? Do we gaze upon the still lifes at Pompeii and imagine Vesuvius, a sister mountain of Santorini's in Eurasia's ever-active cradle of vulcanology, exploding two thousand years ago? Do we dwell on Tambora or Krakatau, or do we perhaps remember the scary movie that we saw at the mall last summer? Who do we ask to paint for us a picture of the Atlantean disaster?

Perhaps Marinatos, who inspired Mavor and others, and who wrote in his famous paper: "The collapse of Thera was a disaster comparable to nuclear war today. Hundreds of thousands of persons could have lost their lives. Cities, ports and villages on many islands and on the mainland of Greece and Turkey could have been washed away or inundated by torrential rains triggered by a spew

of ash. What remained would have been toppled and pounded to rubble by tidal waves. Fleets of ships would have foundered or been hurled many miles inland. Cities on the highlands, at least those close to Thera, would have been rocked and torn by earthquakes. And all the while, volcanic ash would have blackened the heavens, turning day into night, with thunder crashing, lightning searing the sky, and the seas becoming clogged with mud."

Does this suffice? Do we need to imagine Zeus fashioning those thunderbolts, sparking that volcano in the center of the island, pulling ocean waves nearly four hundred feet into the sky, watching the sea pour into the cauldron that once was Atlantis—a cauldron of steaming sea water that is immediately eight miles wide and a mile deep, growing wider and deeper by the half second—watching the civilization sink beneath the roiling, boiling waves?

We do not need to do this, should we choose not to. But we must remember that the Atlanteans did imagine it, just like this—Zeus and all. "Whether or not they were being punished by the gods for their misadventures," Atwater told me, "the important thing is, they *thought* they were being punished. How could they not have thought so? They had been benevolent for so long, and had found themselves blessed. They had then turned avaricious, and look what happens.

"We cannot know what forces were at work that day and night, beyond the natural ones. But we certainly can know that the Atlanteans thought a message was being sent from on high.

"And maybe they were right."

. . . and so could Chile, on its morning after. That, of course, is the hardest time, when you awake and ask, "Who survived? What's next?"

ATLANTIS is called by many the lost continent. Atlantologists see this as a strictly geologic term, for they largely agree that Atlantis as represented by its people—Atlantean influence, Atlantean ways—never vanished altogether.

There were surely survivors of The Cataclysm; Spyridon Marinatos found strong evidence for it, as Richard Ellis recounted: "After Mavor left Greece, Marinatos returned to Akrotiri to continue the excavations. In addition to great numbers of shards, he uncovered a 50-foot-long wall constructed of large stones, which showed a reddish tinge, as if they had been subjected to intense heat. Even though it was buried deep in ash, the wall lay on top of more ash, showing that it had been built after an eruption had blanketed Akrotiri. They demonstrated conclusively that the residents of Thera had returned after an earthquake and rebuilt their settlement."

So some few Atlanteans tried, vainly, to rebuild Atlantis. And then, beyond this local news, there was the Atlantean diaspora.

"THE FIRST major political result of the disaster was the occupation of Knossos by a Greek-speaking dynasty," wrote Luce in *Lost Atlantis*. "Simultaneously came a great westward displacement of the surviving population in search of cultivable land. New sites were occupied in western Crete, and former ones enlarged. The refugees did not stop there." The exodus staggered through Greece, Italy and Sicily as well as Rhodes, Cyprus and Egypt. "But they sailed no longer as masters of the sea, and chief traders of the eastern Mediterranean," Luce continued. "They were now exporting themselves, not their goods."

Luce speculated that in the first wave of forced emigration, a group of Atlanteans may have settled as far away as Tunisia, for a tribe of "Atlantes" was known there in the classical period. Another group certainly went eastward and settled in the coastal strip of southern Palestine, and were later known as Philistines. The biblical prophet Amos (c. 800 B.C.) talks of this migration, coloring the event with a description of vulcanism and inundations.

It is hardly surprising that Atlantean survivors trickled into Europe and Asia. What *is* astonishing is the number of Atlantean colonies discovered throughout the world, and the depth of Atlantean influence perceived by certain archaeologists, anthropologists and others. Among these "others" place even Adolf Hitler, who was convinced that some high priests of Atlantis escaped The Cataclysm by boat and established a colony in Tibet. Hitler theorized that subsequent generations of Atlanteans worked their way from the Himalayan outpost to northern Europe, where they begat the Nordic, or Aryan, race. Hitler was obsessed with finding a pure Atlantean community, and sent Nazi expeditions to Tibet. There they searched vainly for blond, blue-eyed Atlanteans—vainly and ignorantly because, of course, if ever found, the Atlanteans would have looked more Greek than anything.

> SO SOME FEW ATLANTEANS TRIED, VAINLY, TO REBUILD ATLANTIS. AND THEN, BEYOND THIS LOCAL NEWS, THERE WAS THE ATLANTEAN DIASPORA.

WHILE WE cannot blame Ignatius Loyola Donnelly for Hitler's insanity, we can blame him for the idea that Atlantis is everywhere around us. Born in 1831, this Philadelphian is more responsible for the fame and allure of Atlantis than anyone since Plato. His *Atlantis: The Antediluvian World* first appeared in 1882 and has, by now, gone through more than fifty editions. It was a sensation when it appeared; it remains one today.

Which is not to say that it is anything but, as Atwater expressed it to me, "pure nuts," or that Donnelly is anything but a crackpot.

He was an eminent man, though, Donnelly was. A lawyer by trade, he moved to Minnesota and became that state's lieutenant governor, then a congressman. (His career stands as an early example of Minnesota's occasional practice of electing a truly wacky politician, a practice most recently on exhibit in the elevation of Jesse "The Body" Ventura to the governorship.) Having lost his congressional seat, Donnelly poured his heart and soul into a new passion: Atlantean research, or what passed for research in his world. Any scrap of evidence, he threw it in; no coincidence was too small to note. At 490 pages and with scores of illustrations and mountains of "proof," Donnelly's *Atlantis* assaulted the world and, twisting its arm behind its back, wrestled the world to the ground. "Plausible, perspicacious, buttressed

Donnelly: Accomplished man, legislator, celebrity, crackpot— and principal proponent of all things Atlantean

by many curious and recondite facts," pronounced one reviewer, and others were more enthusiastic by far. The book was a phenomenon and started an Atlantis craze; New Orleans, for example, adopted Atlantis as the theme for its 1883 Mardi Gras parade. Never mind that *Atlantis* was a bulked-up hodgepodge of hooey, British prime minister William Gladstone read it and wrote Donnelly a letter of glowing praise. The book could not be ignored. Even Charles Darwin read it, albeit with what he termed a "very skeptical spirit."

Of the five parts in Donnelly's book, four aren't worth commenting upon, but the fifth, "The Colonies of Atlantis," is. Donnelly saw Atlanteans everywhere, around every corner, behind every door, under every bed. Noting, for instance, that many different cultures passed down chaos stories, he decided that all of these societies descended from the first true civilization which was . . . well, you know. He observed that a certain word in Icelandic sounded like a word in Ceylonese, and asserted—on his own—that both words must have come down the linguistic pathway not from the Latin, but from the Atlantean. The madness of Donnelly's method: "There is abundant proof—proof with which pages might be filled—that there was a still older mother-tongue . . . the language of Noah, the language of Atlantis, the language of the great aggressive empire of Plato." So there.

As for Donnelly's colonies, they were everywhere, on every continent, save Australia (opposite page). You couldn't swing a dead cat in Donnelly's universe without hitting an Atlantean.

Again, it can't be overemphasized: Donnelly's *Atlantis* sold like Stephen King, and it put Atlantis on the map. Nevertheless, it was bunkum. The real

ATLANTIS:
THE ANTEDILUVIAN WORLD.

PART I.
THE HISTORY OF ATLANTIS.

CHAPTER I.
THE PURPOSE OF THE BOOK.

THIS book is an attempt to demonstrate several distinct and novel propositions. These are:
1. That there once existed in the Atlantic Ocean, opposite the mouth of the Mediterranean Sea, a large island, which was the remnant of an Atlantic continent, and known to the ancient world as Atlantis.
2. That the description of this island given by Plato is not, as has been long supposed, fable, but veritable history.
3. That Atlantis was the region where man first rose from a state of barbarism to civilization.
4. That it became, in the course of ages, a populous and mighty nation, from whose overflowings the shores of the Gulf of Mexico, the Mississippi River, the Amazon, the Pacific coast of South America, the Mediterranean, the west coast of Europe and Africa, the Baltic, the Black Sea, and the Caspian were populated by civilized nations.
5. That it was the true Antediluvian world; the Garden of Eden; the Gardens of the Hesperides; the Elysian Fields;

1

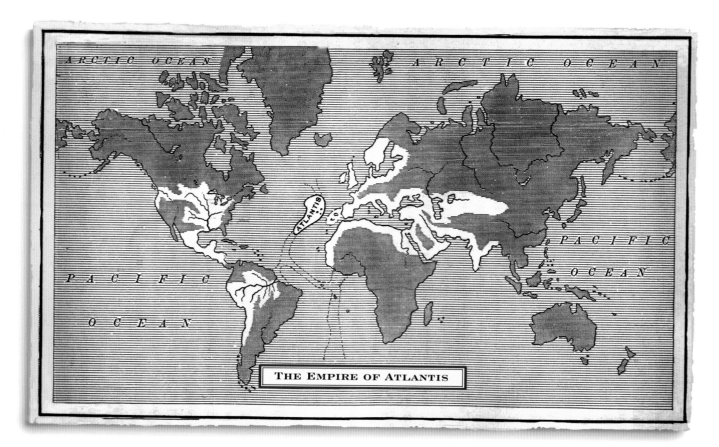

THE EMPIRE OF ATLANTIS

facts of Atlantean colonization, like those of Atlantean language, Atlantean art and all other things Atlantean, are easily grasped: the culture has been thinned over time, precisely as many other cultures have been. As the population dispersed and was assimilated, its Atlantean nature diminished. "Atlantis has all but vanished from the face of the earth's surface," Atwater told me, rubbing that scar of his, the one high on his forehead. "Not with a bang, but a whisper.

"No matter what Donnelly said."

IT ALL BUT VANISHED from the hard, cold *face* of the earth.

But Atlantis would prosper pure in one place—the place, as Atwater might want it said, whence it had come.

How many Atlanteans survived there, at the base of the great, sheer cliffs of Santorini? Two of them on that isolated beach? Four? Was there an Atlantean Adam and Eve, or was it a Noah's ark scenario: a score or more scared creatures huddling on the smoldering rock, rock that was their temporary life raft, rock that would float them until . . .

How many? We'll never know. Because these few Atlanteans, as opposed to Donnelly's millions and Luce's thousands, would leave behind no evidence of new habitation on terra firma. These Atlanteans, frankly, had had their fill of life on land.

As soon as the smoke had cleared from The Cataclysm, as soon as it was certain they had been spared, they began their crawl back into the sea. They, most firmly, set their sights on going home.

> DONNELLY'S ATLANTEAN COLONIES WERE EVERYWHERE. ATLANTEANS WERE BEHIND EVERY DOOR, UNDER EVERY BED. YOU COULDN'T SWING A DEAD CAT IN DONNELLY'S UNIVERSE WITHOUT HITTING AN ATLANTEAN.

DE PROFUNDIS

PART THREE

THEORIES OF DEVOLUTION

How the Atlanteans Adapted

ATWATER TOLD ME OVER AND over and over again: "They had learned their lesson. Those who survived felt they knew what The Cataclysm had been about. They felt a message had been sent. We will never know if these survivors on the beach were princes or paupers of Atlantis. We can't know if they had been guilty or guiltless Atlanteans. We can't know if they had been good and just and noble, or tyrannical and despotic and malevolent. These things are unknown, and don't really matter. What matters is: It is evident from the subsequent behavior of the survivors that they felt Atlantis, their nation, had screwed up. Big time." And then Atwater repeated: "So remember this—they had learned their lesson. That's the key to the whole thing. That's the lesson of Atlantis."

BARBARA MOORE is gazing through thick plexiglass at the New England Aquarium on Central Wharf in Boston, watching a dolphin swoop and swoosh in the water beyond. "Elegant," she says. "Probably a good deal more elegant than your *Ambulocetus*, in fact." She smiles pleasantly. She has made a research scientist's joke.

Ambulocetus is the subject at hand—*Ambulocetus* and other animals like *Ambulocetus*. Moore isn't sure why someone is inquiring about *Ambulocetus*; it is sufficient that her friend, known to us as Atwater, has asked that she be helpful, and so she will be.

"I've been doing some work on yellowtail snapper, and I'm into bluefin tuna right now, not whales," says Moore, who is head of the National Oceanic & Atmospheric Administration's Undersea Research Program and is, currently, working on a project in conjunction with the aquarium. "We've got this tagging study going on with the tuna. My theory is the range of the giant Atlantic bluefin is much larger than we've believed, and I'm trying to prove it. But I've always got a little extra time to think about whales."

She moves away from the window. "*Ambulocetus*, that was the fellow they found in Pakistan, right?

Ambulocetus natans: the swimming walking-whale. Weighed around six hundred pounds when it roamed. That was about . . . what? Fifty million years ago? Still retained its mammal's tail. No fluke yet. And it had immense feet with six-inch toes, and a good hind-leg structure. Short forearms. Probably a lumbering land mammal, but a pretty good novice swimmer. That the guy?"

"That's the guy."

"What about him?"

"Well, what was he? Was he a mammal, or was he a whale?"

"Both. A whale is a mammal. He was a whale, for sure, a whale who had lived the last of his many generations on land and was heading for the ocean. Those hind legs would disappear, those forearms would tuck right in and he'd be a nice, classic whale before too terribly long."

"But why?"

Scientists such as Barbara Moore (inset) are trying to help all the sea's creatures: snappers, whales—by extension, Atlanteans.

"Why what?"

"Why was he becoming a whale?"

"He *was* a whale."

"Why was he becoming a whale—an ocean whale—again?"

"Ask him."

"No, I mean, isn't that going backward—heading from the land into the water? Isn't the classic evolutionary pattern to climb out of the water onto the land?"

"The classic one, maybe. I guess this guy wasn't a classicist."

"Joking aside—isn't it surprising that a mammal who's doing okay on land takes to the water?"

"It needn't be. Maybe there was competition for food on land, a competition he was losing. Maybe there were predators. Early whales were carnivores, but they were still whales—they probably didn't do too well against nastier beasties. Maybe there was drought. Maybe he had been ocean-

> [WHY DID THE WHALE OPT FOR THE SEA? MAYBE HE WAS SIMPLY FED UP WITH LIFE ON LAND.]

inclined all along—or water-inclined. Rather than risk having to get from pond to pond in times of drought, he decided it was better to be in the pond all the time. Maybe . . . well, maybe he was just fed up with the land.

"I'm not being facetious here. These are simplifications, but they could have been the reasons."

Moore, a sharp-witted but nonetheless kind soul, senses my exasperation.

"Look," she says. "You've heard of Stephen Jay Gould, right? He's smarter than me, he's smarter than our friend even—what did he want you to call him? 'Atwater?' That's pretty good. *Atwater*. That's rich.

"Anyway, Gould's great on this stuff. When Atwater told me what the subject was, I knew Gould was the one you'd need." She jots an address on a piece of paper. "Here. Go down to Legal Sea Foods, have a chowder, have a Sam Adams. Then hop a cab out to Cambridge and talk to Gould about *Ambulocetus*. He's expecting you. He'll set you straight."

I do precisely as ordered, and enjoy the beer and fish stew nearly as much as I enjoy Gould's lively telling of recent breakthroughs in evolutionary science. Gould, the Alexander Agassiz professor of Zoology as well as Curator for Invertebrate Paleontology at Harvard's Museum of Comparative Zoology, is, for all his erudition, a vivid and comprehensible teacher. After greeting me genially at his office on Oxford Street, he offers a brief preamble to an exegesis on whale devolution:

"Pliny the Elder, before dying of curiosity by straying too close to Mount Vesuvius at the worst of all possible moments, urged us to treat impossibility as a relative claim: How many things, too, are looked upon as quite impossible until they have actually been effected? Armed with such wisdom of human ages, I am absolutely delighted to report that our usually recalcitrant fossil

The great Roman naturalist and scholar Plinius Secundus (Pliny the Elder), who died in the year 79 while witnessing the eruption of Vesuvius, told us to treat impossibility as a relative claim.

record has come through in exemplary fashion. During the past fifteen years, new discoveries in Africa and Pakistan have greatly added to our paleontological knowledge of the earliest history of whales. The embarrassment of past absence has been replaced by a bounty of new evidence—and by the sweetest series of transitional fossils an evolutionist could ever hope to find. Truly, we have met the enemy and he is ours."

Gould is happy about something. It turns out he is happy about recent discoveries involving *Pakicetus, Basilosaurus* and our friend *Ambulocetus.* As an evolutionist, he had long been frustrated in nailing down proof that land mammals had crept into the ocean and become sea mammals. He and his fellows had long intuited this to be true; Gould, certainly,

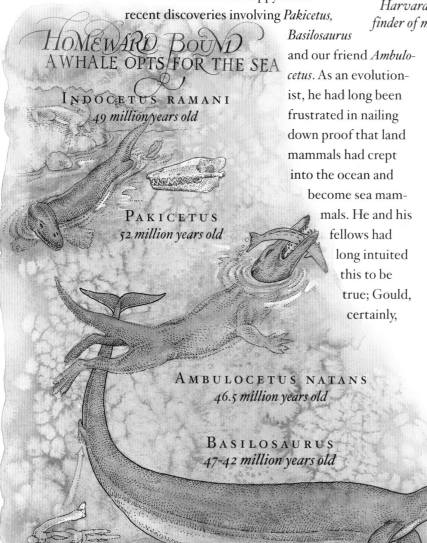

*Stephen Jay Gould,
Harvard professor,
finder of missing links*

HOMEWARD BOUND
A WHALE OPTS FOR THE SEA

INDOCETUS RAMANI
49 million years old

PAKICETUS
52 million years old

AMBULOCETUS NATANS
46.5 million years old

BASILOSAURUS
47–42 million years old

knew it to be true. But they couldn't find the missing link.

And then, "Case One: discovery of the oldest whale." This was *Pakicetus,* so named "to honor its country of present residence." It had the teeth of a terrestrial mesonychid but the skull of a modern oceangoing whale. Next, "Case Two: discovery of the first complete hind limb in a fossil whale." This belonged to the sadly misnamed *Basilosaurus*—the word means "king lizard," though the animal is clearly an early whale.[8] Gould describes the limb system of the fossilized *Basilosaurus* as "a lovely and elegant structure including pelvic bones, all leg bones and nearly all foot and finger bones, right down to the phalanges of the three preserved digits."

Case Three involved *Indocetus ramani,* another early whale with hind legs of a more appropriate size than those of *Basilosaurus.* This seems to excite Gould, but its significance eludes me.

Case Four introduced the swimming walking-whale, old Amby, of whom Gould says with affection: "*Ambulocetus* was no ballet dancer on land, but we have no reason to judge this creature as any less efficient than modern sea lions, which do manage, however inelegantly. Forelimbs may have extended out to the sides, largely for stability, with forward motion mostly supplied by extension of the back and consequent flexing of the hind limbs—again, rather like sea lions."

As mentioned, Gould had been stumped for years by an inability to build a solid bridge between land mammals and marine cetaceans. But with *Ambulocetus,* he and his colleagues finally had what Gould calls "the smoking gun": a walking whale gone swimming. "Some discoveries in science

---

8 "*Basilosaurus* will always be *Basilosaurus,*" Gould says in lamentation. "We do not change ourselves to *Homo horribilis* after Auschwitz, or to *Homo ridiculosis* after Tonya Harding–but remain, however dubiously, *Homo sapiens,* now and into whatever forever we allow ourselves."

are exciting because they revise or reverse previous expectations," he says. "Others because they affirm with elegance something well suspected, but previously undocumented. Our four-case story, culminating in *Ambulocetus*, falls into this second category. This sequential discovery of picture-perfect intermediacy in the evolution of whales stands as a triumph in the history of paleontology. I cannot imagine a better tale for popular presentation of science."

As I thank Dr. Gould for his time, I do not dare suggest to him that there just may be one better tale lurking in the depths of the sea.

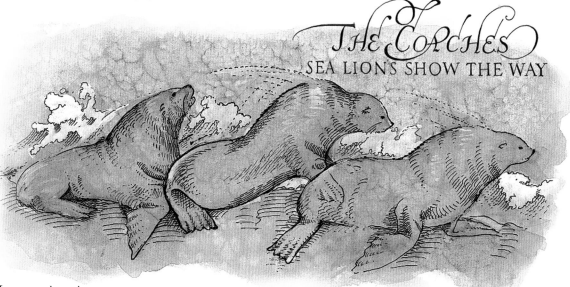

THE COACHES
SEA LIONS SHOW THE WAY

Step by step, inch by inch, sea lions — with fore limbs providing stability and hind limbs providing propulsion — taught early lessons to devolving Atlanteans.

*S*O MUCH TIME spent on whales.

But it is a crucial point: Whales did it, out of some need that we can only imagine. Wild horses have done it, feral cats have done it: they went back. Will Steger's sled dog did it, when she turned from husky back into wolf.

Atlanteans could do it — and would. They, too, would do it out of need, a need that is, by now, apparent to us.

"It's not devolution, really, though that's what some call it," says Mead Treadwell, director of the Institute of the North and the Pacific Rim Fisheries Program at Alaska Pacific University. Treadwell, safely sheltered a continent away, has been a sounding board for some of Atwater's more advanced Atlantis theories. "Animals such as the whale or Atlantean man are *evolving*, no 'de' about it. 'Devolution' is a regressive term. It's an affront, really. We can see why it's used: it appears that the animals are going back three steps, as if they were playing a game of Chutes &

Mead Treadwell, Alaskan scientist, Atwater confidant

Ladders. But while it is true that they are returning to a place they've already been, they are returning as quite different beings, sometimes quite different species. They retain the progress they've made, and they look at their return as another forward step. In fact, as opposed to animals that never left, they can be seen as not stagnant at all, but proactive. They *choose* their environment, even if they do so under some new duress. It's like the bright kid who goes to New York City — 'If I can make it there, I can make it anywhere' — then returns to his hometown and becomes mayor. He's not a loser, he's a winner. He tasted New York, chose Podunk, and he will live in Podunk the rest of his life — with all of the experience, savvy and armor that New York has bestowed.

"Devolution? If you think Atlanteans weren't king of the seas overnight, once they went back, then you're sadly mistaken. You take a loincloth-wearing *Homo sapiens* and drop him among a bunch of shrimp and squid, and he's the big fish in the pond. Immediately. I mean, the halibut's a perfectly nice fish and has some okay instincts, but he's about as bright as a farm-raised salmon.

"Devolution's a pretty insulting term to use and particularly so with Atlanteans. Remember, when The Cataclysm hit, Atlanteans were the best and the brightest the world had to offer. I have very large doubts as to whether the scruffy tribes scuttling about elsewhere at that time could have pulled off such a devolution. But the Atlanteans did."

Eric Widmaier, professor of biology and physiology at Boston University

NOW THERE IS, of course, nothing intrinsically impossible about *Homo sapiens* returning to the sea. Earlier discussions involving wild horses, wolfdogs and Stephen Jay Gould's whale have laid the groundwork. But how could the Atlanteans have pulled off their stunt so fast?

"Because they felt they had to," Atwater told me. "The species has always been adept at responding to evolutionary opportunity— that's why mankind has progressed so very far as rapidly as it has. The Atlanteans used this human instinct, and added to it their uncanny knack for taking clues from other, nonhuman species— a knack that would serve them well once they were back under water."

"Call this guy," he added. This time the name Atwater scribbled on a sheet of paper was Eric Widmaier. "He's a professor of biology and physiology up at B.U.—he's a good

friend. I've told him all about Atlantis, too, just like with Treadwell. He's been looking into this evolution thing for a book he just published. *Why Ducks Aren't Fat*, or something like that."

The book is in fact titled *Why Geese Don't Get Obese: How Evolution's Strategies for Survival Affect Our Everyday Lives*, and the research Widmaier conducted as he wrote the book prepared him to help us with the perplexities of Atlantean biological science. "Pressure leading to evolutionary opportunity only takes you so far, even when you're dealing with a crisis situation such as the one Atlantis faced," says Widmaier during our interview. He is a handsome, animated man, casual in dress and demeanor. He wears jeans and a chamois shirt as he sits in a beat-up old leather chair in his messy office at Boston University. "Plus, you're looking at a seeming impossibility—a multimillion-year-long change speeded up by at least three orders of magnitude. So, yes, you have a problem.

"Let's solve the problem. Now, first, realize that people are by nature fishy. In the womb, even today, we have little gills, and these disappear as lungs form before our birth. So human beings are fishy by nature.

"Second, something might have happened during the Atlantean Cataclysm that served to predispose this group of survivors for their amazingly fast evolutionary leap. Some *X-Files*–type thing. Could the eruption itself have increased the mutation rate among survivors by a factor of a thousand? Maybe. I don't

> "SOMETHING MIGHT HAVE HAPPENED DURING THE CATACLYSM TO PREDISPOSE THEM TO QUICK DEVOLUTION—SOME X-FILES THING."

know. But, well, sure—maybe there were biological aftereffects from a blast that was, after all, far, far worse than a nuclear explosion.

"Another unknown is our friend Atwater's favorite x-factor: their intelligence. Atlanteans were already smart—they ruled the world. There's an aspect of this that is plain but usually overlooked: The world's smartest are also the world's best learners. Archaeologists and social scientists agree that Minoans and Atlanteans were about a dozen generations ahead of their time. They were brilliant students beyond our understanding.

"Now, then—down on the rocks, who would these learners learn from? Animals. Particularly animals they were hoping to emulate.

"Let me tell you what some animals can do. Moths can change their coloration in mere months in order to camouflage themselves against trees darkened by industrial soot. Weddell seals can hold their breath for up to seventy-five minutes. How? Believe it or not, they've learned to shut off parts of their body that they don't need at a particular moment, and so that part requires no oxygen. Fantastic! Do I believe the Atlanteans learned to do that? Well, let me put it this way: I don't believe the Atlanteans didn't learn to do that.

"I know, I know: the eruption occurred less than three thousand five hundred years ago. And judging by ancient historical records from the region and reports of Atlantean colonies elsewhere in the Atlantic, the species was probably amphibi-

ous by A.D. 500, and fully submerged another millennium later: 1500 or so. That's fast, man, that's very, very fast—a geologic eye-blink. But mix in possible mutative effects of the explosion, the world's biggest and best brains, a proven talent for study and achievement and our final, favorite evolutionary principle—need makes speed—and you know what you have? A possibility."

Between arrival and departure in the Northwest Territories—and between fishing and playing cards— Bil Gilbert explained the Need Makes Speed principle.

"NEED MAKES speed": I had heard that before. Several years ago, I was on a month-long camping trip in the far northern reaches of Canada's Northwest Territories. The leader of our four-man group was Bil Gilbert, the great naturalist from Fairfield, Pennsylvania. He had picked an anonymous lake on an old topographical map as a good place to visit. So the bush pilot flew us to the lake, and we put down in early August.

We made camp on a peninsula that extended into the lake. Each morning we would rise early. We would build our morning fire, have breakfast, then hike during the day, taking notes on caribou behavior, grasses, plants, whatever was alive and available. Before dinner, we'd take canoes onto the lake and catch as much char and trout as we chose, to supplement the dry meal we had packed in. After dinner we'd tell stories, play poker, blow harmonicas and drink coffee. We'd sing songs, trying to incorporate the distant wolf howls as harmony. It was as peaceful a time as I've ever known. For us.

Shortly after our arrival, however, I noticed

surface and skimmed two, then five, then twenty-five feet across the small waves. We had only days left in our own time on the lake when one of the youngsters gained a bit of elevation. My heart soared with the bird.

That night, as we watched the northern lights dance splendidly on a black canvas of night sky, the lake froze. But the next morning it thawed, and the ducks went back to their work. They did very well, and the following day even better. On the morning of the day that the bush plane appeared overhead to retrieve us, these still-small birds flew the length of the lake. As our craft lifted off, I was optimistic about their chances, and expressed this sentiment aloud, looking back through the plane's small window.

"Need makes speed," Bil said. "Chancy way to live, but need makes speed."

that four ducklings had only recently been born on our lake. I remarked how late in the season this seemed. Back home, they would have arrived in March, in the spring. Bil corrected me, saying, "It *is* spring. Today is spring up here. Next week's summer. The week after is fall."

It was, as always, fun to watch ducklings grow. Their down was fine and fuzzy; their stumbling, chattering ways as they accepted food was hysterical. I fell hard for the duck family.

The parental unit was anxious; you could sense it. Back home, on Wampus Pond, ducks lolled about during the summer, doing nothing much. The young 'uns grew larger and, eventually, traded their fuzz for feathers. That was about it. But up here, the parents were constantly prodding their young, pushing them about the lake, forcing food, then forcing their offspring to flap. I asked about the unusual behavior, and Bil said, "Nothing unusual about it. It's necessary. This lake will start to freeze in two weeks. If those ducklings can't fly, they'll die. They have to move on, and the parents know it."

Suddenly, we had an emotional stake in the ducklings' progress. Every day as I fished, I silently rooted as the brood lifted off the lake's choppy

> IF THE DUCKLINGS DIDN'T TAKE WING FAST, THEN THEY WERE DOOMED. AS I SAW THE LITTLEST LIFT OFF, MY HEART SOARED WITH THE BIRD.

*C*HANCY way to live: to survive on the rocks for a generation, maybe two, maybe ten, trying to reassemble the pieces of an exploded existence. Certainly the very first of these pioneering Atlanteans took steps back into the water, at least to catch fish (which were then so plentiful in the Aegean that they could be scooped up by hand). Always a culture comfortable with the sea, Atlantis, as these few lost souls now constituted it, started wondering if the sea represented the future.

Then what did they do? As Widmaier says, they started borrowing from animals around them. In trying to discern their methodology, we should look again at a reasonably near mammalian cousin, *Ambulocetus*. What did Amby do early on? He developed horizontal tail flukes. Why this kind of fluke? Stephen Jay Gould suggested during our conversation in Cambridge that the choice probably had to do with Amby's internal mechanics and their similarity to those of other successful water animals: "Particular legacies of terrestrial mammalian ancestry established an anatomical predisposition. In particular, many mammals, especially among agile and fast-moving carnivores, run by flexing the spinal column up and down. Conjure up a running tiger in your mind, and picture the undulating back. Mammals that are not particularly comfortable in water—dogs dog-paddling, for example—may keep their backs rigid and move only by flailing their legs. But semiaquatic mammals that swim for a living—notably the river otter and the sea otter—move in water by powerful vertical bending of the spinal column in the rear part of the body." It's like the butterfly stroke of an Olympic swimmer. Whales, river otters, sea otters, Mark Spitz—and Atlanteans. Gould's succint summation: "The horizontal tail fluke, in other words, evolved because whales carried their terrestrial system of spinal motion to the water."

The horizontal tail fluke evolved because whales—and Atlanteans— carried their terrestrial system of spinal motion to the water.

Understandably the tail flukes came first for Atlanteans too, since swimming was of primary importance. Moreover, it would take far longer for a new breathing system to evolve. Just as whales and other sea mammals need oxygen, so too would aquatic Atlanteans. That would take some considerable time: to rebuild the human pre-natal gill and lung system. So, meantime, the species got its hindquarters in order. It worked on bending the back and on getting those flukes. A transitional phase of the devolution to sea mammal led to a half-man, half-fishlike Atlantean, and this raises the question: Were the Atlanteans what we call mermaids and mermen? For an answer, we look to historical reports.

The first narratives featuring fluke-tailed sea nymphs were related by the ancient Greeks; no surprise there. (Why there subsequently appeared lake princesses in China, the merrow in Ireland, Mélusine of France, Nastasia of Ukraine and the Japanese sea queen will be made clear when we speak of Atlantean undersea colonization.) The lore surrounding mermaids and mermen holds that they were long-lived (compared to most fish, they seemed to be), mortal (of course), musical (compared to most fish, they were), dedicated to the sea (of course) and, while sometimes kindly, often dangerous. To see one, it was believed, was an omen of shipwreck. (But then, for centuries seeing one was so commonplace, any shipwreck could be conveniently blamed on them.) Mermaids and mermen, it was said, lured mortals to death by drowning; Lorelei of the Rhine did this. Mermaids lured youngsters to live with them beneath the waves; one near Cornwall, England, did this, and is remembered as an evil being.

But look at it another way: such deeds could just as easily have been acts of benevolence, or acts of benevolence gone awry. Mermaids and mermen, having tasted life on terra firma, knew just how good life in the sea could be. Some were, perhaps, too zealous in their evangelism. Anticipating that other humans could adapt as quickly as they had been able to adapt, they rushed to entice.

Isn't it touching that they courted the children,

Mermaids and mermen, no matter the culture that is interpreting them, are all Atlanteans under the skin — and under the fins.

offering those who had the longest time yet to live a lifetime of hope and peace beneath the waves?

It's interesting

how many mermaid tales concern the tension between life on the surface and life below, and the merpeople's intransigence in choosing water. "I want to go home," a mermaid named Menana tells the Great Spirit in one Native American legend. The Spirit responds, "It's not that easy to become human again."

Menana begs, however, and the Spirit relents — conditionally. To fulfill her wish, Menana must live for a probative period with humans, until she develops a human body. And then, to become completely human, she must fall in love.

To skip ahead in the story, she does. A suitor named Piskaret tells her of the glories of his native land: big trees, winding rivers, et cetera. Menana is smitten, and suffers all the joys, fears and sorrows of humanity. She agrees to marry, but Piskaret's tribe says no.

They think her strange, inhuman.

Menana is separated from Piskaret. She wanders the forest, singing sadly. She tells her tale to the waterfall—a sympathetic waterfall, of course—and has an epiphany. She rushes to town and tells her friends that she will leave humanity behind and return to her water world. "Why?" they demand. She has no answer to satisfy them.

Back beneath the surface she plunges, soon to be joined by Piskaret, who forsakes land and marries Menana.

This last bit may well be apocryphal: a happy ending for an heroic tale. There is no evidence that mermaids can convert land-dwelling humans, and certainly Piskaret could not have evolved so quickly, so completely. But several themes from "Menana of the Waterfall" are regularly found in other merfolk narratives. "The Sea Nymph and the Cyclops" from Greece, "The Enchanted Cap" from Ireland, "The Serpent and the Sea Queen" from Japan, "The Sea Princess of Persia" from Iran and "The Little Mermaid" from Hans Christian Andersen and Disney all have cross-tide yearnings and merpeople—usually mermaids—with one fluke in either world.

"We can't believe, since humanity is our condition and a world-dominating condition at that, that mermaids and mermen would choose another way," says James L. Gould, professor of evolutionary biology at Princeton and author of *The Animal Mind*. "It's an affront. We just can't get past it. So we tell these tales of how they want to come back to land. Nonsense! They *had* land. They wanted to go back to the water."

Gould, no relation to Stephen Jay, is an etholo-

> ["WHEN WAS THE LAST TIME YOU SAW A MERMAID? IT SEEMS TO ME THEY'RE GONE. THEY'VE EVOLVED PAST THAT STAGE."]

gist—he studies animal organizations, past and present. He is not, it should be noted, an Atlantologist. He continues: "There's another interesting aspect to mermaid tales: they all deal with long ago, with times gone by. There are very few modern merpeople stories. Why is that? Well, when was the last time you saw a mermaid?"

He does not answer. He's teasing us.

Finally, he says, "It seems to me the reason there were so many mermaid stories in the past is because whoever these 'merpeople' were, they have, in our time, disappeared. I can't find that there have been any mermaids and mermen for decades, maybe centuries. It seems they kept bobbing up all over the great wide world for years. Then they either became extinct or—"

"Or what?"

"Or they evolved into something else. Could've happened, you know. If my theory about them preferring the water is right, then each generation grew more scales or a thicker hide. Each generation swam better, moved faster and further, breathed longer under the sea. Each generation had fewer links—links of memory and of romance—with the world of terra firma. They were eventually swallowed up by the sea."

"Thank you, Dr. Gould," I say as I rise from my chair. We shake hands and, as I turn, I remember something that I had been burning to ask of someone, anyone, anyone but Atwater. "Oh, Dr. Gould, one more question. Might some of the creatures have gone one way, and others the opposite way? Might some have gone to sea while others, already halfway toward being merpeople, decided at the

James L. Gould, professor of evolutionary biology at Princeton University

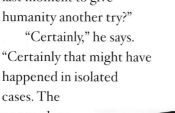

and sea mammals, just as they had the otters or sea lions on the beach, picking up a thing or two here, a thing or two there."

I am sitting on one of the large, granite boulders that line the Maine coast between Ogunquit and Kennebunk on an unseasonably mild January morning, talking with my good friend, the head honcho of the National Fish and Wildlife Foundation. My search for Atlantis has wound back to its starting point. Atwater pointed me in many directions and gave me many new contacts, but when it came time to understand the late chapters in Atlantean devolution and the early years of Atlantean colonization, he said, "Either of the Goulds might be good, but they don't believe in Atlantis like Amos does. At this stage, I'd say you can't do better than Amos."

And so, here I am.

"I don't mean to make it sound so clinically selective as that, like they simply went shopping for attributes," says Amos. "You can't just grow an esca because you want one. But Atlanteans were smart enough to discern that if they followed certain fish into their different domains, then hung out there or established a colony there, well, they could perhaps develop a strain of their own race that had similar characteristics. They got the flukes first, then worked on the lungs by following Weddell seals, manatees, dolphins and whales: mammals most like themselves. Then they started to freelance. They took fliers, they experimented. I think it's safe to say that there's never been any species — any animal — that had so much fun with evolution. We humans use animals all the time for scientific experimentation. The Atlanteans used themselves."

> THE ATLANTEANS DECIDED WHICH CHARACTERISTICS WOULD BE USEFUL TO THEM, THEN SET ABOUT ACQUIRING THESE THINGS.

last moment to give humanity another try?"

"Certainly," he says. "Certainly that might have happened in isolated cases. The great majority would have gone along with the societal consensus, but there are rebels within any group."

I rub my forehead, wondering at the implications of this. "Thanks again, Dr. Gould," I say absently, as I head for the door.

"ONCE the Atlanteans started to get around underwater," says Amos Eno, "they studied lots of other fish

"You can't just grow an esca because you want one," Amos S. Eno points out.

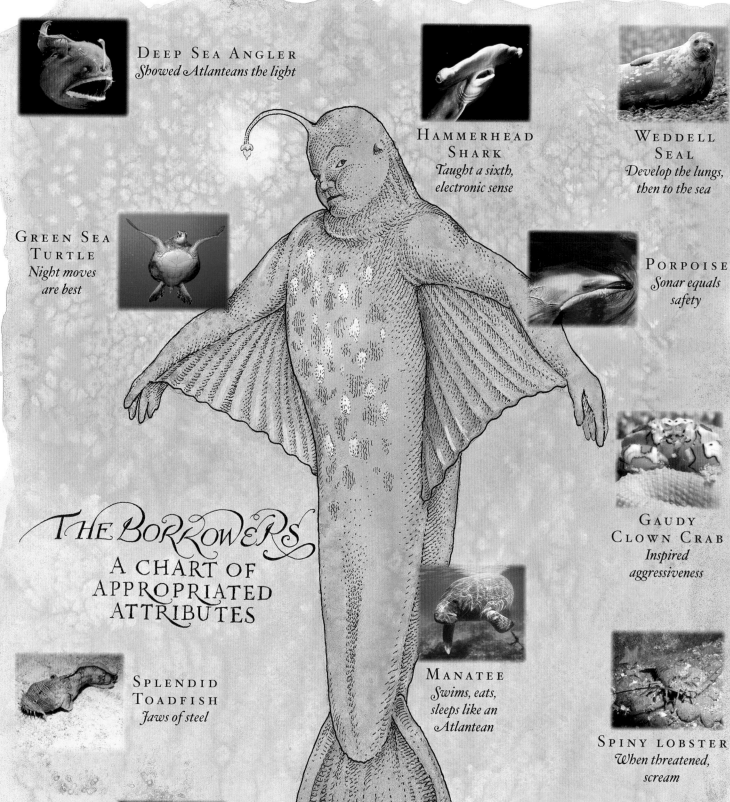

DEEP SEA ANGLER
Showed Atlanteans the light

HAMMERHEAD SHARK
Taught a sixth, electronic sense

WEDDELL SEAL
Develop the lungs, then to the sea

GREEN SEA TURTLE
Night moves are best

PORPOISE
Sonar equals safety

GAUDY CLOWN CRAB
Inspired aggressiveness

THE BORROWERS
A CHART OF APPROPRIATED ATTRIBUTES

SPLENDID TOADFISH
Jaws of steel

MANATEE
Swims, eats, sleeps like an Atlantean

SPINY LOBSTER
When threatened, scream

ORCA
A model breathing machine

TASSELED SCORPIONFISH
The king of camouflage

They wanted to be masters of the undersea universe. It's not that they sought control or dominion; their goal was an aesthetic and technical mastery, a subtle mastery. They wanted no corner or cave of the ocean to be too deep, too dark or too cold for Atlanteans. To this end, they coveted (and eventually developed) sonar capabilities equal to the porpoise's, and electronic sensing instincts like those of the hammerhead shark. Atlanteans acquired these basic defense mechanisms relatively early on. They needed to, because their way of staying alive would rely on an arsenal of duck-and-cover tactics.

The elements that Atlanteans took from near relatives such as whales, dolphins and walruses are obvious. The contributions of other creatures may be less apparent. Here is a sampling of exotic undersea creatures and the particular attributes appropriated from them by Atlanteans:

☆ Splendid toadfish (*Sanopus splendidus*). This oddly shaped, purple, shy creature has inordinately powerful jaws. Now, so do Atlanteans. The fish is named not for its flounderlike appearance but for its unusual croaking sound, easily imitated by almost any Atlantean (whether in an attempt at deception, or just humor, is uncertain).

☆ Tasseled scorpionfish (*Scorpea nopsis oxycephalus*). Atlanteans have tried, with some small success, to incorporate a changeable coloration into their repertoire of defenses. The scorpionfish—and the fairy basslet and a host of others—has certainly been among the models, though it is doubtful that any sea mammal will ever

Aelian, a Roman teacher and poet of the second and third centuries A.D., loved to think about fish. In fact, he was the first to write on fly-casting, as he described Macedonians catching trout with artificial flies.

SEA RAM

"The head of the male sea ram is bound with a white band, like a diadem," wrote Aelian, who was one of those smart Roman scholars, but who was, in this case, mistaken. He was surely describing an Atlantean, its esca aglow.

achieve the palette of reds, yellows and greens that this creature enjoys and employs.

☆ Gaudy clown crab (*Platypodiella spectabilis*). An habitue of the Caribbean, this tiny fellow—less than an inch across—is brave beyond its size. Says Amos Eno, "I think the Atlanteans learned from species such as *Platypodiella* that there are very great advantages to being bold in the deep."

☆ Spiny lobster (*Panulirus argus*). Another Caribbean native, this shy crustacean can scare the bejeezus out of predators with a high-pitched scream. In his book *Beneath the Sea*, Mark Blum, a diver who had heard *Panulirus's* cry, wrote that it was a truly "alarming sound, somewhat like the sound of rosin being rubbed against a violin string." Atlanteans now mimic that sound.

☆ Green sea turtle (*Chelonia mydas*). While not exactly exotic, this other large pacifist taught the Atlanteans a most valuable lesson: Go by night. Turtle babies, hatching from eggs that have been buried in beach sand, emerge after dark so as to avoid predatory birds, reptiles and fish. Mature turtles, too, find the ocean a safer place to travel during the midnight hours. Atlanteans and sea turtles: oversized, amphibious, sweet, vulnerable survivors.

BECAUSE they have taken on hallmark characteristics of several different species, Atlanteans have often been misidentified. Richard Ellis wrote in *Imagining Atlantis:* "Some two hundred years after Christ, the Roman scholar Aelian (A.D. 170–230) wrote *De natura animalism*, in which he discussed an animal called the sea ram (which many have heard tell but few know the natural history), said to be found in the straits between Corsica and Sardinia. 'The head of the male sea ram,' wrote Aelian, 'is bound with a white band, like a diadem, one might say, of Lysimachus or Antigonus or some other Macedonian king.'"

Another sighting, and misinterpretation, came in 1976, when none other than Captain Jacques-Yves Cousteau, the twentieth century's greatest undersea explorer, went to Santorini and descended in his diving saucer. Documenting the expedition in his 1981 book *Searching for Atlantis*, Cousteau wrote pessimistically, "If by some miracle there were vestiges of Atlantis at the bottom of this crater, we surely would have no chance of finding them; the debris of 35 centuries would have buried them." Still, he saw something wholly unexpected, which he took to be extremely rare fish known as regalacs, "very-deep-water fishes called 'king of the herrings' by the ancient authors." Cousteau described a creature that was unique, exotic and oddly elegant: "Their long serpentine bodies are laterally flattened, and covered with little brown spots. The odd dorsal fin looks like a Japanese fan. On its head there are plumes made of fin spines, and under the body are two long, threadlike ventral fins. Their very long dorsal fin extends from the nape to the tail."

Ellis assumed that the explorer had indeed seen "a school of oarfish, *Regalecus glesne*," and then he elaborated: "The oarfish is actually one of the rarest and most mysterious fish in the world, and because of its length (as long as twenty-five feet) and the bright red 'plumes' on its head, it has been held

Jacques Cousteau, latter-day Aelian, saw an Atlantean from his diving saucer and called it an oarfish.

responsible for many sea serpent sightings. This appears to be a rare record for the Mediterranean, and the first case anywhere that I know of where they are described as traveling in schools."

"I WOULD suggest," counters Eno, "that there was no sighting in the Mediterranean of oarfish. The length could be reasonably accurate—Atlanteans are large, certainly, if not twenty feet. Any discrepancy could be put off to deep-sea illusion. And look at the other characteristics reported by Cousteau. Traveling in schools: an Atlantean trait. Mediterranean: the native habitat. You tell me which is more likely: a first-ever sighting of a school—a *school!*—of *Regalecus*, wandering far outside its natural

MATURE MALE ATLANTEAN

Christopher Columbus presumed he was among Atlanteans in the new world.

Aegean—on land and in the sea. Well, now, the world was their oyster."

ATWATER counseled when I returned to Cape Cod with news of my illuminating conversation with Amos: "Watch out for that 'princes' stuff. Be careful with the 'colonization' idea. Again, remember: Atlantis had been spanked. Sure, Atlantis colonized. We know Atlanteans colonized. But they never again took over someone's land. They were a different bird than the one that had been been hit by the volcano. They were kinder, gentler Atlanteans."

It must be true. There is no evidence of any fish or sea mammal species being wholly displaced by an intruder—overthrown, so to speak. We find encroachments in the historical record, and there are depletions caused by mankind (through overfishing, pollution), but there are no fish wars. The Atlanteans were squatters. They wandered, and settled. They didn't push their way in; they didn't push anybody out.

But, oh, did they travel—and in doing so gave rise to all those different answers to the question, "Where was Atlantis?"

PLATO, though he was clearly thinking of Santorini, situated Atlantis in the Atlantic, and by the time explorers and scientists went looking for it in recent centuries, there was plenty of circumstantial

habitat, or Atlanteans in the very waters where they originated? And the bright plumes? Just like Aelian's 'white band, like a diadem' on the head of the 'male sea ram,' I'd say. It is surely the Atlantean esca, aglow. It seems certain Cousteau saw Atlanteans."

The esca—the headlamp—was a crucial development, and represents a massive advantage to the Atlanteans. The esca is an outgrowth of the spine, with a luminescent bulb on its bony end. Atlanteans certainly developed theirs at the deepest depths, for it is there that escas are prevalent among angler fish. The fat, ugly black devil fish (*Melanocetus johnsonsii*) has a luminescent esca, as does its close cousin, the triple wart sea devil (*Cryptopsaurus cauesi*). For the Atlantean, what better defense, what better device for movement—either within a region or around the globe—could there be? "The esca allowed Atlantis to roam," says Eno. "The nation's princes had already shown their colonizing instincts in the

evidence to indicate that Plato had been right. Some of this evidence was on land, and is most probably tied to the worldwide exodus of Atlanteans and Minoans that, though overblown by such as Donnelly, indisputably occurred. Early in the Age of Discovery, in the fourteenth century, the Spanish discovered on the Canary Islands men who were said to be larger than other humans and similar to western Europeans of 35,000 years earlier. The islanders' stone buildings, the ruins of which can still be seen, had been laid out in perfectly circular neighborhoods. Some historians have placed the original Atlantis in the Canaries.

When the Portuguese "found" the Azores, the islands were deserted, but again there were remnants pointing to earlier habitations by an advanced European civilization. When Columbus went a-finding aboard the *Santa Maria* in 1492, he carried with him the Benincasa Map, which featured three mysterious islands floating in the central Atlantic: Antilia, the "savage Island" and a third that went unidentified. Were these Atlantis? Columbus wondered. He hoped so, for he had been advised before departing that he could stop at some of the vestige islands of Atlantis to re-stock for continued voyage. When Columbus made landfall in the Bahamas, he surely felt he was walking among people who were descended from Atlanteans.

Donnelly, the crank who saw wheels within wheels, thought that Columbus himself came from Atlantean stock, and wrote baldly, "When Columbus sailed to discover a new world, or to rediscover an old one, he took his departure from a Phoenician seaport, founded by that great race 2,500 years previously. This

BACK TO THE FUTURE
THE DEVOLUTION OF ATLANTEAN MAN

MEANS OF ESCAPE, MEANS OF SURVIVAL: *desperation leads to the first dive.*

NEED MAKES SPEED: *legs fuse and lungs develop in the blink of an eye.*

CREATING A SPLASH: *half man and half fish, the merpeople gain fame.*

THE SEA MONSTER ERA: *hairless, webbed, unique and inscrutable, Atlanteans are not pretty.*

THE COMPLEAT ATLANTEAN: *fully devolved, the species roams the seven seas.*

Atlantean sailor, with his Phoenician features, sailing from an Atlantean port, simply reopened the path of commerce and colonization which had been closed when Plato's island sank into the sea."

It is not easy, sometimes, being an Atlanto-pologist.

DONNELLY ESPOUSED what remains a popular theory: that the deep-sea Mid-Atlantic Ridge holds the key to Atlantis's original location and its sinking: "All these facts would seem to show that the great fires which destroyed Atlantis are still smoldering in the depths of the ocean; that the vast oscillations which carried Plato's continent beneath the sea may again bring it, with all its buried treasures, to the light." Since the Mid-Atlantic Ridge of suboceanic mountains — indeed volcanic, indeed still active — was not examined until after World War II, Donnelly's passage does seem remarkably prescient.

But there's a problem with this theory: the vulcanism associated with the Mid-Atlantic is actually building land up, not sending it down. Iceland is a product of this volcanic chain, and the whole ridge is slowly rising toward sea level rather than receding further from it.

Which is not to say that Atlanteans don't live on and about the ridge. Many of them do, which serves to prop up various location arguments.

"Atlanteans love thermal vents," says Eno during a follow-up phone call. "Who wouldn't?"

"See, what happens is, in the ocean valleys, lava oozes down from the volcanoes of the Ridge, and then cracks as it cools. Into the cracks goes the cold sea water, which is heated by the magma beneath. Out shoots this super-hot water, which is extremely rich in minerals — the whole process is

fantastically life-producing. The vents look like smoke pouring from deep-sea chimneys, because the water temperature is so extremely different, and also because of the nutrient swarm. Around these vents massive communities of bacteria, shrimp, mussels, snails, clams, tubeworms and fantastic fish thrive.

"Now, Atlanteans are not vegetarian. They might have gone pacifist on us after The Cataclysm, but they do eat seafood. So they, too, congregate at the vents.

"In 1997, Woods Hole was part of a big vent-finding expedition in the Atlantic. Ask Atwater to give you info on that one."

Giant Tube Worms

SOUP'S ON
AT THE ATLANTEANS' DEEP SEA BUFFET

Cold Sea Water

Chimney

Lava

Ocean Floor

Magma

Super-heated Water

Galápagos Rift. Since then, fifty vents worldwide have been examined.

As Atwater's file indicated, at each of these vents bountiful sea life has been found, along with things that remain unexplained. Not least among these mysteries was the phenomenon variously called "a curious phosphorescence" (1984 Australian South Pacific study), "a bright luminescence" (1987 Japanese study of North Pacific vents) and "unexplained fluorescence" (1993 Canadian/U.S. study of the North Atlantic). In addition, reports of vent exploration indicated that some of the marine life had apparently set up more sophisticated living systems than might have been anticipated. For example, this from the Canadian/U.S. study: "Caves and caverns were clearly inhabited, most probably by bottom-dwelling angler fish, as a fluorescence was evident from within, this fluorescence presumed to be from escas. Metaphor: Caves appeared to have 'lights in the windows.' Could not positively identify all the many elongated fish thereabouts due to deep-sea darkness."

The 1997 EC–Woods Hole team made nearly a hundred dives in all. The scientists were principally interested in population genetics and movement, how shrimp, crabs and other animals (they dared not mention Atlanteans in print) migrated from one island to another along the undersea mountain chains: ridge-hopping vent to vent from one Azore to another, for instance.

It was just southwest of the Azores, in fact, that the teams hit paydirt on July 10. At 36°13' north latitude and 33°54' west longitude the French sub-

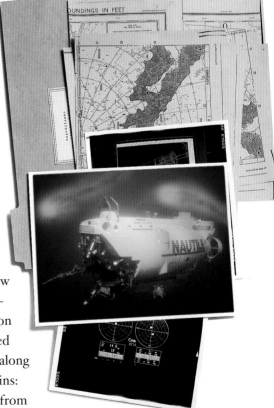

"YOU'LL LOVE the irony," Atwater said as he handed over the materials. "Let's make that ironies, plural. The submersible that was used on this mission was the *Alvin*, which our old Atlantophile James Mavor helped design. And the surface ship from which the *Alvin* descended was R/V *Atlantis*. I think it's beautiful that Woods Hole, which is covering up all this other stuff, names a research vessel *Atlantis*. You can say what you want about those boys, but they do have a sense of humor."

A synopsis: In 1997, a European Commission survey team of scientists went out upon the Atlantic with a Woods Hole team in a cooperative effort to study vent fields, vents representing a relatively recent topic of research. It was only in 1977 that humans first laid eyes on a vent, that one in the

mersible *Nautile* found what is now believed to be one of the largest volcanic vent fields in the Atlantic. A hundred yards square, the area had what was described as "a forest of more than one hundred smoking vents." Researchers named the field Rainbow because on the day of its discovery, a beautiful rainbow appeared over the ocean. Of Rainbow's sea life, an unidentified scientist typed, "Among the larger species, very large fish—oarfish?—six to twenty feet, lth. (mammalian shape?), escas apparent. Traveling in schools. Spd: fast. Feed on shrimp, plankton, microbes."

In the right margin of that page, in pencil, was a single, scribbled word—"*Atalante*"—followed by two question marks.

"Not mine," Atwater said when asked. "I don't speak French."

Francis Bacon was not the first and would hardly be the last of very bright, very serious-minded people to say for certain that he could pinpoint Atlantis.

*F*RANCIS BACON, who some say wrote the plays attributed to Shakespeare, assumed in the early seventeenth century that Plato's "opposite continent" across the "real sea" was, in fact, North and South America combined. He thought that Native Americans ("Amerindians," he called them) were Atlanteans. He, as Donnelly would after him, saw similarities in Amerindian language and the tongues of Europe and Asia.

Albert Hermann, a German historian and geographer, thought that a dried-up marsh in Tunisia—the Chott Djerid, which had once been a Mediterranean bay—was the site of ancient Atlantis. Local Tunisian legends tell of a powerful kingdom thereabouts that had been swallowed by the sea.

Jurgen Spanuth, another German, believed that Atlantis had been a northern continent, and was now beneath the North Sea. During a 1953 expedition off Heligoland, he found Stone Age flint tools and undersea walls of red, black and white.

Rachel Carson, the brilliant American naturalist and author of *The Sea Around Us* and *Under the Sea Wind* as well as *Silent Spring*, once asked rhetori-

cally, "As the hidden lands beneath the sea become better known, can the submerged masses of the undersea mountains be linked with the fabled lost continents?" She, too, had a North Sea theory of Atlantis: during the Ice Age, an area emerged as land which, as the ice retreated, first became an island and then, as the sea rose, ultimately disappeared. Dogger Bank, sixty miles from England and approximately 250 miles from Spanuth's Atlantis of the North, is that land now, submerged. Once there may have been men there, Carson wrote, and " perhaps in their primitive way they communicated this story to other men, who passed it down to others through the ages, until it became fixed in the memory of the race." Carson called Dogger Bank "the lost island."

Imagined locations for Atlantis, in fact, are as varied as the people proposing them. French anthropologists found Atlantis in the Yucatán and in other places throughout Central America. Arthur Poznansky found it in the stone city of Tiahuanaco,

Bolivia. German archaeologist Leo Frobenius found it on the coast of Nigeria, where the Yoruba sea god Olokun still looks a lot like the Greeks' Poseidon. Colonel P. H. Fawcett, who disappeared during a South American hunt in 1925, saw Atlantis in the large stone cities of Brazil. Flavio Barnieron, an Italian naval officer, asserted that artifacts, records and Atlantean ruins will surely be found beneath the Antarctic ice, while Count Byron Kuhn de Prorok scoured the Sahara for years searching for clues to Atlantis that he *knew* were buried there.

In the Pacific, too, there were islands, now vanished. Lemuria was one, Mu was another. James Churchward described the latter in his 1926 book, *The Lost Continent of Mu*, as "a great rich land . . . watered by many broad, slow-running streams and rivers, which wound their sinuous ways in fantastic

Rachel Carson, crusading naturalist, locater of lost lands

curves and bends round the wooded hills and through the fertile plains."

Atwater told me: "Churchward said he was decoding ancient Chinese texts, but he was really mimicking Plato in an effort to turn his Mu into Atlantis. He needn't have bothered. Of course Atlantis was Mu. And Atlantis was Lemuria. And it was—it *is*—Dogger Bank. It is off Brazil and is off the Azores and off Bimini and off the Bahamas and Heligoland. On terra firma, Minoans roamed the world, dropping pieces of Atlantis. And under the sea, their cousins swam far and wide, doing the same.

"You can find Atlantis wherever you like, and you will never be wrong."

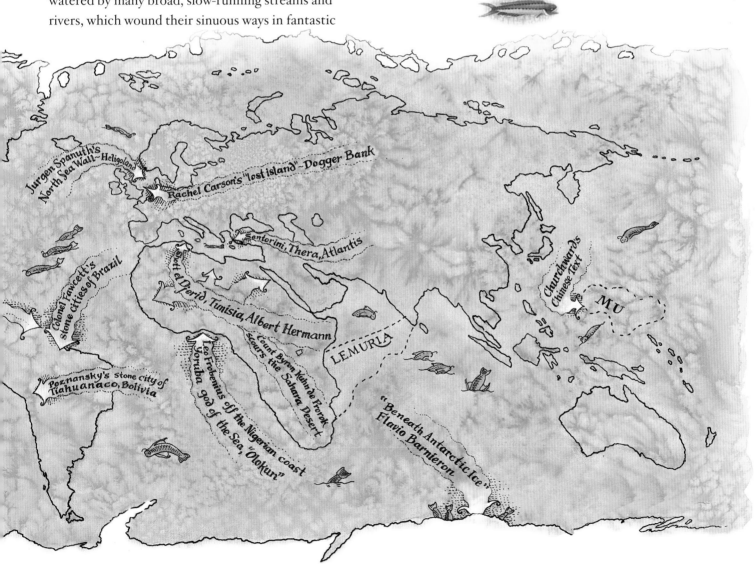

PART FOUR

EDEN REBORN

Atlantis in the Modern World

ATWATER TOLD ME: "ATLANTIS is at its zenith. It has been for a century or more. The early chapters of its undersea incarnation were filled with trials — trial and error on the devolutionary road, trial and tribulation as colonies were established throughout the seven seas, trial by fire as the Atlantean republic came into contact with modern man. Each new trial that did not kill Atlantis made Atlantis stronger. Eventually, Atlantis emerged a fully confident nation again, and today this strong, moral nation is not just sitting on its flukes: It is a very pro-active community." He paused, then added ominously: "Which is not to say that all is well in Atlantis. Threats remain, threats posed by humankind. Will Atlantis ultimately survive?" Atwater left the question unanswered.

THE IDEA "schools of fish" takes on new meaning when speaking of Atlanteans, for Atlanteans have, through the centuries, spread their philosophy and learning far and wide. More than a hundred years ago, Heinrich Schliemann found ancient Egyptian papyri in St. Petersburg, Russia, that read, "Pharaoh sent out an expedition to the west in search of traces of the land of Atlantis from whence, 3,350 years before, the ancestors of the Egyptians arrived carrying with themselves all of the wisdom of their native land." Of course what neither Schliemann, a great believer in Atlantis, nor Pharaoh, also evidently a believer, nor the writers of similar statements in the famous Harris papyri at the British Museum in London, nor any pre–twentieth-century Atlantologist knew or suspected: the Atlanteans carried forth their wisdom not only over the land, but beneath the sea as well. "This," Atwater told me, "is a strictly modern conclusion, scientifically arrived at. Woods Hole is really the only place where the big picture has been put together."

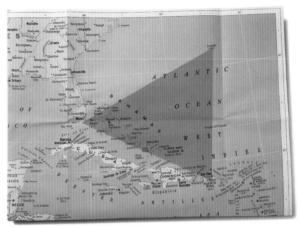

The Bermuda Triangle

This picture of Atlanteans on the move throughout the oceans was painted for me by Atwater's testimony and that of the various sources he put me in contact with, and also, significantly, by the myriad confidential reports, memos, maps and photographs in Atwater's files. Atwater's true name may even have been on some of the forms—I don't know, and I never pressed the point with him. Mavor's name was absent. I suspect that because Mavor was very publicly the "Mr. Atlantis" of Woods Hole, he kept arm's length from the Atlantis Project, perhaps serving as a senior advisor or counselor, a wise head.

I felt certain that Atwater's fingerprints were everywhere on the materials as I pored over them, but, again, I was reluctant to force the issue.

Besides, as I delved further into the mystery of Atlantis, questions concerning which scientist was behind which opinion seemed far less important than the facts behind the amazing story itself. The facts, taken in whole, seemed to sketch an epic narrative: the story of a chastened race that returns to a certain kind of power.

But were they facts? I so wanted to make sure, at every stage, that I was dealing with facts. I often reminded myself: "This is not *my* information. It's Atwater's, and I'm hearing the story as Atwater wants it told. How do I know if it's true?"

And then, one night, my inquiries took a turn.

MANY theorists have put forth the Bermuda Triangle region of the Atlantic as the long-ago site of Atlantis. They, too, find a linchpin in Plato: "[Atlantis] was subsequently overwhelmed by earthquakes and is the source of the impenetrable mud which prevents free passage of those who sail out of the straits into the open sea." Aha! Preventing free passage of ships. Obviously the Triangle.

On the night in question, I mentioned this theory to Atwater—and he exploded, if not like Santorini, then at least like Vesuvius. "There is no greater travesty in Atlantology!" he thundered, fairly shaking the clapboards of the little cottage. "It's an absolute corruption of the lesson of Atlantis, and that's particularly tragic since the lesson was so painfully learned in the first place." His face was red; he was rubbing his forehead furiously as he limped around the room.

"Calm down!" I urged.

"The Bermuda Triangle!" he went on, disregarding me. "The Bermuda Triangle implies Atlanteans are cruel—as if they do these wicked things for

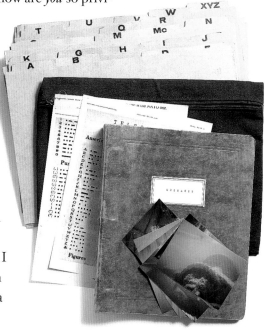

kicks. They sink boats and bring down planes like little kids pulling wings off flies."

"Atwater, I was only wondering—"

"Look," he said, interrupting a second time. With some effort, he sat down on the footlocker before my chair, then leaned forward, took off his spectacles and looked deep into my eyes. "These were smart people. They had been the smartest creatures on earth, and now, undersea, they still were. And those who had been spared by the gods turned the nation toward benevolence. The Bermuda Triangle, which I think is a lot of baloney anyway, is evil. Intrinsically evil, therefore anti-Atlantean. There are Atlanteans in the Bermuda Triangle I am sure, but all other evidence would indicate they're against it, not for it. It's like all that violent imagery in Atlantis movies, all that war-mongering. Atlanteans would hate that image. They *do* hate it—we know they do. They hated *Waterworld*. They sunk the set."

"What are you talking about?"

"Nothing," he said abruptly. "You wouldn't understand. You're still not ready."

"I'd try to understand," I said, "but this is getting crazy. You're talking about the Bermuda Triangle, then stupid movies. You're ranting. And then you say things like 'all other evidence would indicate' and 'we know what they feel.' What evidence? How do you know—how are *you* so privileged to know—what Atlanteans are really like?"

He said nothing for what seemed like forever, sitting sullenly, rubbing his right knee (he had chronic pain in both legs, Amos had told me, even as Amos had advised against raising the subject with Atwater). Atwater sat there, rubbing his knee, and said nothing at all. It was suddenly so quiet in the cabin that I could hear the surf rumbling on the seaward shore of the Cape a

mile away. It was eerie, this pause, and I grew very, very tense. Moments ago, I had been angry. Now I was nervous.

Finally, back in control of himself, Atwater asked, "In going through the materials, have you come across the names Larkin and Robinson?"

"I don't think . . . Yes—yes, I have. Just last night, in a file I couldn't figure out. I was going to ask you about that tonight."

I REMEMBER even now.

The previous evening had been cold and rainy on the Cape. Atwater was away, and I set myself for a good, solid work session. I came upon the file labeled "Messages," having just finished the "Merpeople" file and, earlier in the evening, the "Manatee" study (similarities to Atlanteans, et cetera). I opened this next, rather fully crammed envelope labeled "Messages," and pulled out a few typed pages. Lots of loose notes fell out, notes that had been handwritten by someone other than Atwater—I could tell because I had grown used to his rather horrible penmanship in the hundred files that I had already finished.

The typed pages *had* clearly been written by Atwater; they sang with his singular flair. Their message, confused as it was, was delivered not only obliquely but offhandedly. As he did during our conversations, Atwater mixed prosaic science with

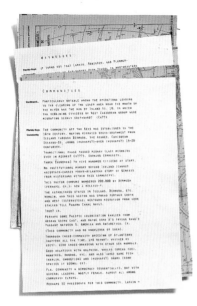

moments of high passion—shockers and stunners, theories and assertions. A brief excerpt: "The community off the Keys was established in the 16th century, having migrated south-south-west from Iceland through Bermuda, the Azores, Caribbean Islands— St. John's (perhaps?)—over (perhaps?) 15–20 centuries. Transitional phase passed midway (last mermaids ever in Azores? Ck???). Growing community. Three to five hundred citizens at start. No institutional memory be-yond Iceland (cannot ascertain— cannot prove—Atlantean story of Genesis from historians within this community). This sector commune numbered 200,000 by Bermuda (per-haps. ck.); now 1 million-+. The established states in Iceland, Bermuda, etc. remain, and this sector has spread farther south and west (interesting: west-ward migration from here stalled till Panama Canal built. True? ck. Perhaps some Pacific colonization earlier from Aegean going east, and maybe some A's trying Drake's Passage between S. America and Antarc-tica. Ck. This community had no knowledge of such). Thorough cross-community breeding of Atlanteans (happens all the time, L+R report; whither my sect?); zero cross-breeding with other sea mammals. Good relations with dolphins, whales (orcas too), manatees, dugong, etc. and also large game fish (marlin, swordfish) and (perhaps?) shark (some species it seems; ck). Fla. community a demo-cracy (essentially), but with several leaders, mostly female, almost all among community elders. Perhaps 50 presidents for this community. Larkin + Robinson report that . . ."

And this was the reference that I remembered.

bruce t. robinson
robbie . . . "right here on our show!" . . . oceanographer . . . sports lover

As FOR THE scribbled notes, they were a mess. Clearly, the typed account was some sketch by Atwater of an ideal, extant Atlantean community relying, I supposed, on Platonic rules of law and whatever scientific evidence was at hand. Maybe the notes were some thoughts on this by Larkin and Robinson, whoever they were—researchers? scientists?—and perhaps all of this would be the bedrock for a more elegant narrative of Atlantis that Atwater would write in the future. As I say, I couldn't figure it out.

But the notes: they were a mess. Many had nothing but apparently meaningless and unrelated phrases like "lovely day" and "150 feet" and "azure" and "shipwreck, 1765." On others were scrawled some of the locations that Atwater had mentioned in his typed account: Bermuda, the Azores, Iceland and so on. In addition to the notes that featured words and numbers—"1," "7," "11" and so forth— were other notes that included what looked like Morse code. I could tell what it was by the dots and dashes, but having never learned the system, it all remained Greek.

To me, at least.

Now, TONIGHT, when Atwater asked if I had heard of Larkin and Robinson, it all came back: last night, the rain dripping through the roof into a pan providing an odd metronome to the Mahler I had put on the CD player. It all came back.

"They were referenced in that file I couldn't figure out, Larkin and Robinson . . ."

"That, my friend, is the most important file in there, by a long, long distance," said Atwater.

"It is?"

"You can skip the rest. You can skip N through Z. Well, you might get a kick out of 'Titanic.' But if you've read 'Messages,' then you're holding the keys to the kingdom."

"You will explain, of course."

"I will explain," said Atwater. "Of course."

⟜

ATWATER SAID to me, and I say to you: "Now, then, are you sitting down?"

Michael S. P. Larkin and Bruce T. Robinson, lifelong friends now in their mid-forties, have for years coordinated their vacation schedules to include at least one shared scuba-diving adventure annually. "Their way of staying in touch," Atwater said. Strictly recreational divers, they preferred Bimini as a destination because life on that island could be just as adventurous as life in the water.[9] Bimini was not a year-in, year-out proposition for the boys, however. They dove in the Gulf of Mexico, off the Pacific Northwest, off Brazil. They did the Great Barrier Reef of Australia one year when they were feeling flush, and tried the Aleutians one year when they were feeling restless. They did Hawaii a few times, and Florida a couple of times.

"That's where it happened," Atwater said matter-of-factly, "in Florida, off the Keys. That's where they made contact."

It happened in 1994, and many of Atwater's details regarding the undersea world of Atlantis were learned from Larkin and Robinson's account. They had no idea what they had stumbled upon during those strange dives—although they knew pretty quickly that they had stumbled upon *something*—and they quietly funneled their information through a friend to the scientists at Woods Hole.

"You'll need to talk with him, too, a guy named Barry Plummer," said Atwater. He went on to tell me that Larkin, Robinson and Dr. Barry Plummer have "no formal link to the Institute—none whatsoever—and they're as upset as I am that this thing

9 "Robinson's a Parrothead," Atwater explained, which did not help me. "A Jimmy Buffett fan," he added. "Robinson's been known to sing 'Margaritaville' in public. He's married now, but when he was younger, I guess he was quite a piece of work."

is being buried. I can set up a meeting for you."

"Here?"

"No, it can't be here. Larkin and Robinson won't come out to the Cape anymore. I'll set it up. I'll let you know where."

⟜

THERE ARE few places more lonely and barren in mid-January than Nantucket Island, twenty miles off the Massachusetts coast. And so it is arranged that here I will sit down for both days of a weekend with these three men, and hear their tale. Atwater does not attend.

It turns out that Larkin, Robinson and Plummer were classmates at Chelmsford High School in northeastern Massachusetts, and have remained close. Robinson at one time wanted to be an oceanographer: he had dreamed of Woods Hole much as the young Atwater had. But after graduating from Colby College in Maine, life and marriage took him down another path. Today he works for the Fred C. Church Insurance Company and still lives in Chelmsford. Larkin went to Bates College, in Lewiston, Maine, close to the coast, and is now a hospital therapist; he was living on the Florida panhandle, in Panama Beach, the year of the fateful dive. (He has since relocated, and chooses not to divulge his whereabouts.) Plummer is a psychologist

Robinson (opposite), Larkin (top) and Plummer had been friends since childhood. They were still close by the time Larkin and Robinson went diving off the Florida Keys (below) in 1994, and that's a crucial point. As a team, they would deliver critical information about Atlantis, past and present.

in private practice in Cumberland, Rhode Island. He also serves on Brown University's faculty.

Larkin and Robinson are the divers. Plummer joins them for tennis and the occasional ski weekend, but never on their deep-sea adventures.

I tape-recorded my sessions with the trio, of course. For the historical record, I should note that these discussions all occurred at Gloria and John Kilmartin's house, in the island's center, where we were alone. (The Kilmartins opened their cottage as a favor to their friend Atwater, even though it was deepest off-season.) Larkin, Robinson, Plummer and I chatted during morning coffee and through afternoon beers, dinner and late-night port. The three friends seemed to enjoy themselves immensely; they did a lot of catching up during the weekend, talking about wives and kids and so forth, even as I tried to keep our focus on Atlantis.

Michael S. P. Larkin, conversant with Atlantis— and Atlanteans

Only the crucial parts of our discussions are included in the following dialogues.

We are on Nantucket Island, off Massachusetts, then, and Larkin speaks first.

LARKIN: Bruce showed up on Tuesday and we drove down to Tampa, then on Wednesday out to the Keys. The first day of our charter was Thursday, and we headed out just after dawn. A brilliant day.

ROBINSON: A nice day, a nice day. Sun glistening on the ocean. Pretty calm surface. Looked like you could see clear to the bottom, which, of course, is a Keys illusion. You can't, but it looks that way.

LARKIN: Fly Fantosi skippered the charter. I'd used him before. Little guy. Little guy with a big family, so he's always safe, never takes undue risks. We anchored maybe two miles offshore, in very deep water. Not far from Bimini, actually—just keep Bruce away from Bimini at night, and he's fine. Superb water for fish. We were psyched.

ROBINSON: Nice water. Very nice water. Nice fish.

LARKIN: I guess it was noon when we started the dive. Bruce?

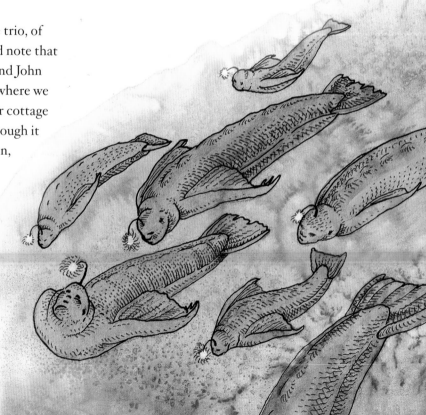

ROBINSON: About noon, yeah. I'll tell you, the entire trip to that point—the weather, the smooth sea—had been so ordinary, I really didn't expect anything special or weird as I went over. I was anticipating a very nice dive, that's about it. Maybe hoping to glimpse some big fish, maybe a marlin, barracuda, something. But other than that, just looking for colors. A pleasant first day.

LARKIN: I was leading . . .

ROBINSON: We alternate.

LARKIN: We do. This day, I was leading.

PLUMMER: So what? You figure your're leading, you retain the film rights?

LARKIN: We haven't gotten to you yet. Shut up. So anyway . . . I was leading. I think I got us in trouble because the day was so clean, so easy.

ROBINSON: Very nice day.

LARKIN: We followed some fish, we

> "IDIOT THAT I AM, I'D FOLLOW OLD MICHAEL ANYWHERE. HE WENT DEEPER, SO I WENT DEEPER."

went deeper and deeper.

ROBINSON: Idiot that I am, I'd follow old Michael anywhere. It was lovely, though, translucent at that depth—a hundred feet. Right, Mike? It had an otherworldly feel.

LARKIN: Yeah, you're down there in inner space . . .

PLUMMER: "Inner space," my granola-crunching friend? You can see why I don't dive with these guys. Listening to 'em talk about it is like listening to Yanni.

LARKIN: Shut up, he explained asecond time. So anyway . . . I guess I brought us down to a hundred ten feet, which isn't necessarily smart. You have to be cautious at that depth because nitrogen narcosis—

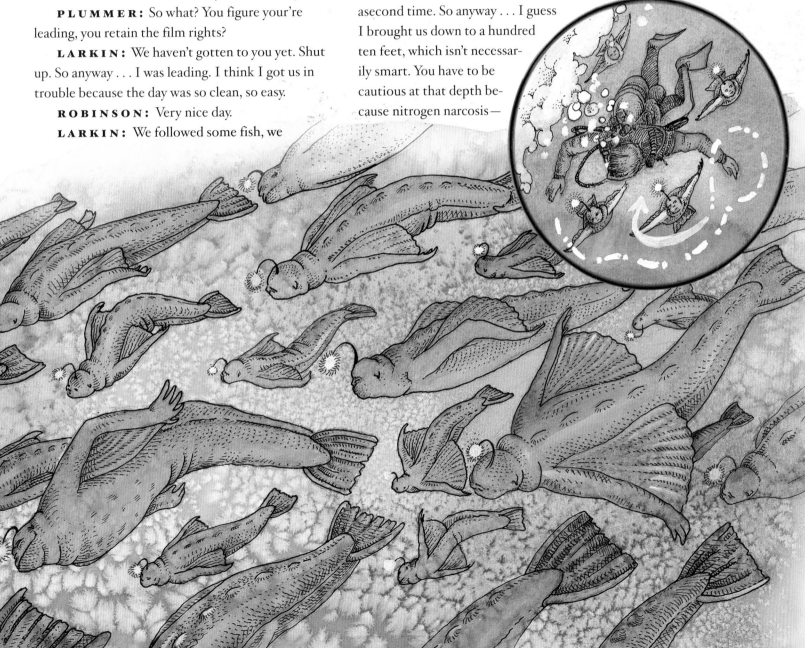

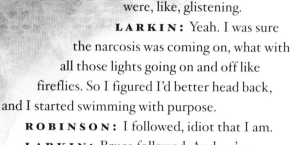

ROBINSON: Too little partial air pressure to oxygenate the blood. Rapture of the deep.

LARKIN: Yes, my poetic friend, rapture of the deep can come on pretty suddenly, particularly if you rise too fast. And it sneaks up on you: you don't feel dizziness coming on, but all of a sudden things are dizzying. You can see down fifty feet in that water, this weird light. Left and right are azure. You feel drunk. You're in a globe, like one of those snow globes, and your whole world, your very existence is defined by—

PLUMMER: Man, oh, Manischewitz! Calm down my friend!

LARKIN: Okay, your existence is entirely weird. Let's leave it at that.

PLUMMER: Let's.

LARKIN: And so we have.

ROBINSON: Before going further, though, I've got to tell you what we saw. As Mike said, you can see fifty feet down. And somewhere down there I saw these big manatees—longer, slimmer than usual. A whole lot of them, maybe fifty. And they

Bruce T. Robinson, oceanographer wannabe, teammate in close encounters

were, like, glistening.

LARKIN: Yeah. I was sure the narcosis was coming on, what with all those lights going on and off like fireflies. So I figured I'd better head back, and I started swimming with purpose.

ROBINSON: I followed, idiot that I am.

LARKIN: Bruce followed. And we're swimming along, and I started hearing this clicking, sort of clicking and whirring and humming. The clicking: I figured dolphins were near. Maybe even whales, though it's not their habitat necessarily. But dolphins made sense.

ROBINSON: Suddenly, Mike turned around. He started swimming the other way.

LARKIN: Well, what happened was, something told me, "Turn around." Something told me that I had become disoriented. And, sure enough, the anchor was the other way. We found it in fifteen minutes, once I'd turned around. Before, I'd been heading for Cuba. We would have drowned for sure.

PLUMMER: You'll love this next part.

ROBINSON: The next part is, however, true enough. That night, at dinner, Mike and I were talking about our near thing and Mike confided, "It wasn't just that I sensed we were going in the wrong direction. It was those exact words in my head—'turn around.'" And I said to Mike, pretty sarcastically, "Oh, yes, of course, some fish said it. Some fish yelled 'Turn around!'" And Mike said nothing. The next day, we went to the same spot, and everything became clear.

LARKIN: You see, some fish *had* said "turn around." That's what the fish had said.

ROBINSON: Not a fish, exactly, as we now know. And not exactly *said* it.

ON THE DAY of the second dive, Robinson and Larkin noticed the manateelike creatures again and heard a lot more clicking and humming. Then, suddenly, the cacophony among the fish stopped, and one voice was heard, quite distinctly. It was very firm and measured. With its short clicks and longer hums, it was, as well, easily translatable.

ROBINSON: We're both not only certified to dive, we've passed basic seamanship. It was clearly Morse code.

LARKIN: Well, it certainly *seemed* like Morse code. Only . . . Well, when we started to translate in our heads, and realized it made sense—perfectly lucid passages, stitched together elegantly, darned near eloquently—well, then we realized it *was* Morse code, and we figured we were going crazy.

ROBINSON: We realized something very, very, very, very strange was going on.

LARKIN: I remember looking at Bruce, mask to mask, at about eighty feet down. He looked thrilled much more than he looked terrified.

ROBINSON: And Mike was over the moon. He was bug-eyed. He clearly wanted to shout, to scream. But that's always tough, at that depth.

ONCE THEY'D SURFACED, the two men immediately agreed to put in for another week's vacation each, extending their stay. They chartered Fantosi's boat for six days beyond the initial five, giving firm instructions to "hit the same spot, exactly, every day." For obvious reasons, they will not divulge longitude and latitude, nor even which of the Keys they were approximately two miles from.

Their story is that they conducted twice-a-day conversations with the Atlanteans, never coming very near them—they didn't pet them, as people do

> "IT SEEMED LIKE MORSE CODE. WHEN WE TRANSLATED IT IN OUR HEADS, WE CAME UP WITH PERFECTLY LUCID PASSAGES."

dolphins, but got close enough to identify which creature was speaking (hence the numbers, or "names," in Larkin and Robinson's scribbled notes). They learned a lot of Atlantean history, much of which has already been fed to us by Atwater. And they learned about the Atlantean nation's current, ubiquitous condition. The state of the Atlantean union is strong, say Larkin and Robinson. Strong, but precarious.

They left the Florida Keys not knowing what to do. Larkin, a bachelor, told no one. Robinson elected to tell not even his wife:

LARKIN: Bruce and I don't have a whole lot of scientist friends.

ROBINSON: Fact is, we don't have any.

LARKIN: But we had Barry. He was sort of a scientist. More important, he was like a brother.

ROBINSON: We called him up in Rhode Island and told him we had to get together. Within a month of the dive in Florida, we were up in North Conway, New Hampshire, ostensibly on a ski weekend. We got him drunk, and lowered the boom. He took it in good spirits. Then he woke up

in the morning and said, "What the—"

PLUMMER: "Heck." I said, "What the heck was that all about?" So that day, we had this strange skiing day at Wildcat Mountain, where every trip up the chairlift one of them co-opts me. I never rode alone. And I was kind of captive, and they laid all this stuff on me. I said, "I want to see your notes." And that night, they showed me the notes. The first notation of any kind was Mike's, and it said:

— • — • — • — • / • — •
— • — — — • • — — • — • •

(Translated: "Turn Around.") And there were many more.

LARKIN: Barry was—

ROBINSON: Nonplussed.

PLUMMER: Yes, I was nonplussed. Or was it plussed? Anyway, it took about a month of talking and reading—not just their stuff, but stuff about sea mammals, communication skills thereof, so on and so forth—before I started to think that something truly odd had happened to my dear friends down there in Florida.

ROBINSON: It was Barry who first made contact with Woods Hole.

PLUMMER: Yes. Mike and Bruce had no contacts, but I knew several guys who worked there. It's only about an hour from Cumberland. The doctors from Brown play softball against those guys, and I had gone to that summer camp for eggheads they hold each year. So I called those guys and said, "Look, I think there are some pretty strange fish swimming off the Florida Keys. These friends of mine went down there and . . ."

LARKIN: Suffice it to say, the Woods Hole folks weren't surprised.

PLUMMER: True. They were not surprised. And they were way, way more receptive to hearing

![Dr. Barry Plummer portrait]

Dr. Barry Plummer,
friend of the witnesses,
link to Woods Hole

everything Mike and Bruce wanted to tell them than I ever imagined they would be.

UNFORTUNATELY, we must make this long, if beguiling, story somewhat shorter than it deserves to be. Plummer helped Larkin and Robinson codify their notes and observations; then the two divers were debriefed on Cape Cod by Atwater, with Plummer attending. Plummer, Larkin and Robinson came away with five clear impressions: The subject, amazingly, was Atlantis; Woods Hole knew something about Atlantis; this information was going no further than the room in which they sat; Atwater himself, at least, was a straight shooter; there had never been contact made with Atlantis before (though they inferred that Atwater had been trying).

"All of that's true," Atwater told me, after I had returned from the Nantucket summit. "Not before, not since—not even by Larkin and Robinson—has there been contact established. They are correct that I have tried. Others here have tried as well. But news must have spread within the Atlantean community that someone among them had talked, and that quite enough had been said.

"You know what? I agree with that," he continued. "The Florida community said enough—almost precisely enough, in fact. The Florida pod confirmed what we needed to know, and then went back to being who and what they are. Which is nothing more nor less than really cool sea mammals with one highly refined social conscience."

> "THE INSTITUTE WAS NOT SURPRISED BY MY INFORMATION, AND WAY, WAY MORE RECEPTIVE TO HEARING FROM MIKE AND BRUCE THAN I EVER WOULD HAVE IMAGINED."

order to communicate by imitating dolphins, which, with the high degree of folding of the cerebral cortex, possess a brain, and probably a language system, most comparable to those of primates. I'm certain that clicking was the way Atlanteans communicated, and then when they started hearing ships and submarines talking to one another with the clicks and hums of Morse code—the aural equivalent of dots and dashes—then it was probably a very simple task to decipher the language with their human intelligence. Morse code is a universal language, so what better vocabulary for the Atlantean community with its global reach?

"I'm sure this is why we haven't heard from them before now. Until the twentieth century and the phenomenon of ocean-going vessels communicating beneath the waves, Atlanteans had no possibility of finding a common-ground language with which to approach humans. I'm sure they had already learned the dolphin's native tongue and the whale's, maybe even the manatee's and the dugong's. But after devolving past their mermaid/merman phase, there was no way they could talk with *Homo sapiens*—until Morse code."

Bil Gilbert, author of the landmark 1961 book How Animals Communicate, *says Atlanteans "could have mastered Morse code in a semester."*

⟡

𝓐 QUICK TANGENT before proceeding, for there is one question that, I'm sure you will agree, needs answering: How in the wide, wide world did Atlanteans learn Morse code?

"Pretty easily, I'd bet," says our naturalist friend Bil Gilbert, the man who helped explain for us the need-makes-speed evolutionary principle. Gilbert, author of the landmark 1961 work *How Animals Communicate* as well as a half dozen other books on history and natural history, says, "You've told me that they're expert mimics, with their impressions of the spiny lobster's scream and the splendid toadfish's croak. So they probably learned to click in

𝓕ROM WHAT they told us—or, rather, told Larkin and Robinson—Dr. Barry Plummer, an experienced psychologist, was able to sketch a profile of Atlanteans, albeit an admittedly superficial one. In a follow-up phone call after the Nantucket Island summit, he helped us to understand the nature of the beasts:

"They're friendly, first of all. With Mike and Bruce they got into all their history of being a corrupt people when they were on the island over there—off Greece, was it?—and then being punished and learning the error of their ways. They've got these kind of George Washington, Thomas Jefferson figures in Atlantean history, who sort of preached what the nation should become. Fishy

founding fathers. No Declaration of Independence, of course—nothing written down. All oral tradition. And then they found their way underwater, and eventually started to prosper. You're right when you say they learned to live at all depths—or Atwater's right. Whoever's saying so, is right. They learned to survive in the deepest realms by following whales, expelling most oxygen from their lungs at the surface and instead using oxygen combined with the hemoglobin of the blood and the myoglobin of the muscles for their long-dive supply. This allows them to avoid decompression sickness and caisson disease—'the bends.' The fact of figuring this out allowed them to feel good about themselves, and about their prospects. They gained confidence. They started to teach, to pass on their better instincts. They told Mike and Bruce, though this might have been bragging, that dolphins and manatees were not nearly so friendly, nor so communicative or smart, before they started mingling with Atlanteans.

"They built communities, which probably accounts for all of those cool, mysterious ruins that have been found at depth. The first ones looked like Greece or Rome, buildings like

the Parthenon. They tried building on ice floes, in coves. Eventually, they devolved to the point where they realized it was better simply to go as fish. They've been living in caves for a long time.

"They are, by our terms, heroic. No doubt about that. What they have done with distressed ships big and small has been absolutely amazing. Sailboats lost off Long Island or *Titanic* itself, doesn't matter. They're here to help, is what they figure. They feel they are atoning.

"They are also funny, in a way. The thing with the *Waterworld* set is hysterical, if you ask me.

"If you want to understand them quickly, I would say this: they are not unlike the Irish. They've had high times with ancient, sometimes ruthless kings and chieftains. They've been laid low by an oppressor, in one case Zeus and in the other the English. They have a mourn about them—I

distinctly sensed a mourn about the Atlanteans, a somberness, despite their current healthy state. They live in a beautiful land, but a land that has terrible as well as lovely weather. They are survivors. They have done their part to save civilization—the Irish monks by copying the great works into things like the Book of Kells, even as the Dark Ages swept Europe, and the Atlanteans in their everyday efforts. They are poets. They are tale tellers, *seanachies*. They allow you to believe in all things, from fairies and elves to life ever after. They have experienced a diaspora: the Irish are everywhere on the planet, and so are the Atlanteans. Both races—Hibernian and

Atlantean— have a wink in their eye and a song in their heart.

"And they are in their heyday. There may be peace in Ireland, finally. And, these days, Atlantean eyes are smiling, too."

INTO THE BREACH
ORCAS AND ATLANTEANS ARE BREATHTAKING ON THE SURFACE

*T*HEY ARE and they aren't.

Fantasists have long taken an interest in Atlantis, and what's interesting about Larkin and Robinson's report is that Atlantis has lately had a keen reciprocal interest in how its own nationhood is portrayed. "Careful how you phrase that," Atwater counseled. "Atlanteans obviously had no way of knowing what Jules Verne was saying about them, or about some of the nonsense spewed by Cayce and Blavatsky, for instance. But, yes, in recent years the citizens of Atlantis seem to have formed opinions about such things as violent movies about them, or misrepresentations of deep-sea life—at least according to Larkin and Robinson's testimony, and some pretty strange circumstantial evidence."

To backtrack: Verne loved the idea of Atlantis, and was as specific as an historian in pinpointing the place—not to mention every bit as accurate as self-professed historians such as Donnelly. In *20,000 Leagues Under the Sea*, published in 1870 (twelve years before Donnelly's *Atlantis: The Antediluvian World*), Verne had Nemo and Arronax exit their submarine, the *Nautilus*, at 16°17' west longitude and 33°22' north latitude, and make their way toward a "light shining brilliantly, about two miles" distant in the Atlantic. They climb a mountain, which turns out to be a volcano whose activity illuminates the

KINDRED SPIRITS
LIKE THE IRISH, ATLANTEANS HAVE KNOWN MAJESTY AND MELANCHOLY

deep and reveals a city with "roofs open to the sky, its temples demolished, its arches in pieces, its columns on the ground." The ruins remind Arronax "of the stately architecture of Tuscany," for not only is there a city, but "Farther on were the remains of a gigantic aqueduct; here were the encrusted remains of an Acropolis, with the floating forms of a Parthenon; the remains of a quay, also, vestiges of an ancient port on the shore of a vanished sea, which had given shelter to merchant ships and craft of war; farther still, the outlines of crumpled walls and long lines of wide, deserted streets, an ancient Pompeii buried beneath the sea." An ancient Pompeii which Nemo quickly identifies as Atlantis.

Verne was a remarkable seer: his *Nautilus* submersible might as well have been the prototype for vessels that were still half a century off, while the streets and harbors of his Atlantis are extraordinarily like those of Akrotiri, even though the Santorini/Akrotiri theory wasn't on the table in Verne's day.

Sir Arthur Conan Doyle was a seer, too, as were

Jules Verne was a fantasist with a feel for facts.

Edgar Cayce and Helena Petrovna Blavatsky, all of whom painted vivid if wildly varied portraits of Atlantis. Doyle, at least, confessed that his was fiction. Yet he alone among the three came close to the real thing. In his 1929 novel, *The Maracot Deep*, the creator of Sherlock Holmes sent three characters—Holmes not among them—deep, deep into the Atlantic—26,700 feet down, to be precise. There they discover a community populated by—surprise!—humans. Atlanteans.

These sea-dwellers live in an undersea bubble and remember a long-ago life in "a glorious rolling country" ruled from a capital that was "a wonderful and gorgeous city upon the seashore, the harbor crammed with galleys, her quays piled with merchandise, and her safety assured by high walls with towering battlements and circular moats, all on the most gigantic scale." This paradise, however, was laid low by a cataclysm after experiencing general societal debasement. Yadda, yadda. A few who had shrewdly planned ahead were able to sink within the bubble, thereby preserving the race. In Doyle's narrative, the Atlanteans escape their confinement and, elsewhere undersea, confront

The seer Edgar Cayce saw all worlds linked, and linked ultimately to Atlantis.

In a scene from Verne's first edition of 20,000 Leagues, his heroes approach Atlantis.

none less than the devil himself, who admits to having seeded the original "orgy of wickedness" that led to Atlantis's fall. He tempts them toward a reprise, but Professor Maracot, our hero, makes like Holmes and outsmarts old Beelzebub. The book is a hoot and eminently forgettable, but it does make one wonder: How did Sir Arthur Conan Doyle know that the Atlanteans were down there? How did he know that they wanted to repent?

Cayce and Blavatsky make one wonder, too: Where did they get that stuff? Cayce claimed to get it from the past and the future, from spirits living and dead. Through 1,600 "life readings," he determined that about half of his subjects had lived previous incarnations in Atlantis. Cayce's Atlantis experienced a cataclysm (whose didn't?), and his survivors spread their intellectual wealth throughout ancient Europe and Africa. (The Atlantean Hall of Records is buried beneath the paws of the Sphinx, claimed Cayce.) Cayce located Atlantis near Bimini, and said that the lost nation's largest island, Poseidia, "will be among the first portions of Atlantis to rise again. Expect it in '68 and '69." Well, those years came and went with no new ground afloat near Bimini. But it is a measure of Cayce's fame and allure that several costly expeditions were launched in that part of the Atlantic in 1968 and 1969, and some of them claimed to find things—undersea walls, a bunch of once-inhabited caves—that proved the master right.

Madame Blavatsky had her adherents as well. The famous psychic visited America in the 1870s, during a time when the country was in thrall to spiritualism. Teaming with psychic investigator

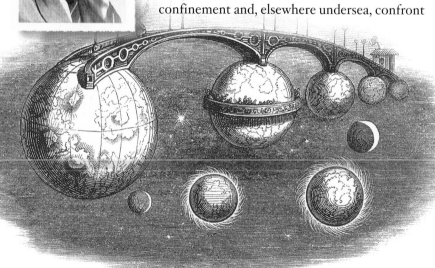

Henry Steel Orcott, Blavatsky formed the Theosophical Society (the name of which combined the Greek words for god [*theos*] and wisdom [*sophia*]). Among many, many other things, Madame claimed that spirits from the Orient told her of the lost lands Atlantis and Lemuria. Atlanteans, she stated, were descended from Lemurians, whose continent sank earlier—millions of years ago, in fact. When Atlantis experienced its own hard times, emigrants made their way to Asia, where they begat the Hindus. With Blavatsky on the scene in the late nineteenth century, forwarding these fantastic theories, it becomes easier to see how America fell so hard and so quickly for the romance and pseudoscience of Ignatius Donnelly.

But then again, maybe the allure of Atlantis was simply irresistible in and of itself. Maybe the story's magnetism derives from its own profundity, its moral core. Maybe the staying power of Atlantis has nothing to do with Blavatsky, Cayce, Donnelly, or even Larkin, Robinson and Atwater.

Perhaps another famous writer and visionary of the late nineteenth and early twentieth centuries—one who never did get around to conjuring the breadth and depth, flesh and blood, of Atlantis—said it best. "There is magic in names and the mightiest among these words of magic is Atlantis," wrote H. G. Wells. "It is as if this vision of a lost culture touched the most hidden thought of our soul."

BLAVATSKY, WHO SEEMED to willfully disregard what pass as facts in the temporal world, was by no means the last to have sport with Atlantis. Sir Gerald Hargreaves, a British judge and amateur composer, wrote a truly bizarre light opera

Bubble-headed Blavatsky said spirits from the Orient told her of Atlantis and Lemuria.

called *Atalanta: The Story of Atlantis* during World War II. The thing was never staged, but Hargreaves's splendiferous paintings of his prospective sets stand as wonderful representations of just how weird things can get with Atlantis. Weird like Hollywood—and that, of course, can get truly weird. Perhaps the most famous film on the topic was *Atlantis: The Lost Continent*, released in 1961. "It has a potboiler plot, a cheesy-looking volcano and lots of minotaurs," declared Atwater, in his thumbs-down film-critic mode. "It also borrows all of its crowd scenes from *Quo Vadis*. Miss it if you can." No better is *Undersea Kingdom*, an installment in the old Crash Corrigan series. "At least watchable for unintended humor is *Siren of Atlantis*, made in 1948 and based upon the French silent film *L'Atlantide*," said Atwater, still the critic. "Maria Montez as the title character bears no resemblance to an actual Atlantean."

In a way, every mermaid picture ever made, from Esther Williams extravaganzas in the 1940s and '50s up through *Local Hero* (1983) and Daryl Hannah in *Splash* (1984) and on to John Sayles's wonderful, mysterious *The Secret of Roan Inish* (1994), has concerned itself, at least obliquely, with Atlantis. So, of course, did *Waterworld*, the

Arthur Conan Doyle, seen in his study, painted an eerily prescient picture of an undersea nation of Atlanteans.

phenomenally expensive, glitch-plagued Kevin Costner epic about oceanic survivors of an apocalyptic cataclysm. That production was obviously Atlantis-inspired, and evidently Atlantis found out about it.

"The Atlanteans never knew what Cayce and Blavatsky and the other crackpots were saying about them," Atwater said late one night as we casually batted bits of Atlantiana back and forth. We were sipping Macallan 18, I remember, and enjoying a warm fire in the grate. Its orange light was the only illumination in the cabin that evening as a February nor'easter beset the Cape, the snow building a thick frosting on the dunes and bringing down power lines from Providence to Provincetown. "How could they know what was being said, being speculated? But 'round about World War II, they started getting wind of certain things. They sure knew there was trouble at that time. Here"—he hunted on the low wooden table before the fire—"where's that 'Messages' file? . . . Here, look at this," he said, thrusting a paper toward me.

It read:

•——•—•—• / ———
—• / —•—•••• / ••—••
••—•—• / —•——••
•—•• / —•—•—•—•••
• / •—•—•••— / •—•—
•—•—— (Translated: "War on, yes? Fifty-sixty years past? Why?")

"And this." He handed me another:

—•—•——••—— / •

Most images of Atlantis in film have ranged from the tacky to the terrifying. Above is a scene from Siren of Atlantis. *Below are stills from* Atlantis: The Lost Continent *and (bottom)* Undersea Kingdom.

•••—••• / •—•—•—
•• / •—•—•— •••
•—•••—•—• / —•••
•••—•—— •—• / —•
——•••—•—•—
/ •—•—•••—•—
•— / •—••—•——

(Translated: "Trouble in Pacific thirty years past. Why?")

"And this."

••—•—• / ——••
—•••—••—•—•—• / ••
—• / —•••• / —••—
—•••—•••—••—•
/ —•—••——•••• / •

——•—••—••• / •—————•—•—————••—••••—•
— / •——•••—•—— (Translated: "Ice melting in northern oceans; water warmer. Why?")

"The Atlanteans didn't know about Cayce, but with Morse code and bombs and all the new ships and stuff, they've been right on top of modern happenings in the ocean."

"Yeah," I said, swirling my small glass of scotch. "They sank *Waterworld*."

"They sure did."

I laughed. I scoffed, is what I did. "Now, how in the world do we know that?"

"It's in the messages," said Atwater, leafing through the pages, handing one over. "See? They came upon this big thing in the Pacific. They watched for a while from a safe distance. Whatever it was—lots of humans, lots of construction—it was clearly violent. There was fighting, or practice fighting, every day. Shooting. They figured someone was going to launch some assault on the seas. I mean, just look at

Waterworld—it's this big doomsday thing. Goodness knows the Atlanteans have had enough of doomsday, enough of catastrophes. So they see this big floating island, which turns out to be the set—but they don't know that—and one night, with those jaws of theirs, they chew through the cables. They sink the set! They make sure no one is aboard to get hurt; then they sink the set.

"Larkin and Robinson spent way too much time talking with them about it since, let's face it, it's not really of cosmic importance. It's a movie. But it was just such a riot, they kept coming back to it.

"It's funny," Atwater summed up. "Every depiction of Atlantis has had some violence, from Crash Corrigan down to *Waterworld*. They all still think of Atlanteans as mean and warlike. I figure nobody's ever going to film the truth. A movie with nice heroes? A movie with sweet Atlanteans? No violence? It's just not as good a story, is it? It's not box office, *bay-bee*."

WATERWORLD was a movie. But *Lusitania* was real life. *Titanic* was real life (before *Titanic* was a movie, that is).

"Look at this one," Atwater said later on the same raw winter's night that was warmed, for us, by fire and whiskey. "Take a look at this."

And I did:

• — / • • • • • • • • • — — • / — • • —
— — • — • • / — • • — • • • — • • • • — • •
— • — • — / • — — • / • — — • • • • • • • /
— • • • • • — • • • — • — • — (Translated: "A ship named *Titanic*. We were there.")

"How did they know the name?" I asked.

"The name was on the boat, and the boat went down. A lot of debris in the ocean by then, and they

THE *WATERWORLD* SET WAS BESET BY PROBLEMS. PROBLEMS CAUSED BY STEALTHY ATLANTEANS?

surely had figured out the relationship between letters and code by that point. By that point, they're speaking passable English, I figure."

But in any event: the Night to Remember is one remembered by Atlanteans. As with *Lusitania*, as with *Wydah*, as with the S.S. *Central America* off Panama in 1857 and the U.S.S. *San Diego* off New York at the turn of this century, Atlanteans swarmed to help. "Larkin and Robinson spent two whole days talking to the Atlanteans about the shipwrecks," Atwater said solemnly as he stared into the dwindling fire, his legs stretched out straight before him. "They were fascinated by the shipwrecks." He stretched, rose and put another log on. This one was birch. "Let's have some pyrotechnics," he said. He gazed at the rising, dancing flames, the birchwood crackling. "People are always fascinated by shipwrecks, by heroics, showy stuff like *Titanic*," Atwater said as he stood there. Then he looked at me and added with a smile, "That's okay, I guess."

"*FROM WHAT* I understand, even as the great ship's nose began to dip toward the water,

ever so gradually, strange lights and strange beings were seen in the waves," says Charles Hirshberg, author of *The Tragedy of Titanic*, during an interview in Greenwich Village subsequent to my discussion with Atwater. "At that time, of course, there was little panic among the passengers—most refused to believe *Titanic* could sink. The ship's officers were growing anxious. They knew what the others didn't, that *Titanic*'s lifeboats would accommodate barely half of those on board. But the passengers them-

selves were clear-eyed when they reported lights in the water. Most of them thought it was a reflection of the billions and billions of stars. It was, as we know, a brilliantly clear, cold and moonless night.

"From what I understand, what followed was a storm of suffering, one that has been remembered in a kaleidoscope of images, some true, some imagined. What stands out is how many survivors reported later that they had been miraculously saved. I'm not talking about Kate Winslet here. I'm not talking about some movie babe getting lucky. I'm talking about a multitude of miracles.

"From what I understand, there was a theory that silver-bearded Captain Smith was some kind of angel, that he was bobbing in the waves clutching an infant in his arms. Just as death's icy fingers begin to close around him, he is spotted by a lifeboat.

As a contemporary account put it— I've got it right here—'When the small boat went to his rescue, Captain Smith handed up the child but refused to get in the boat himself. Pushing himself away from the lifeboat, Smith ripped off his lifebelt, threw it from him and slowly sank from sight.'

Charles Hirshberg,
Titanic *scholar*
of titanic intellect

"From what I've learned, that's pure fancy. The only part that might be true is the lifeboat. At least one member of *Titanic*'s crew thought he saw Smith clinging to one. But the infant and the suicidal gesture were concocted, probably by an imaginative crewman. And why? To put an heroic human face on the inexplicable. Lots of infants, lots of children, women and men were finding their way mysteriously into lifeboats that night, guided or pushed by unseen hands.

"Now, from what I understand, Atlanteans are prehensile. True? They've retained their hands and fingers in all stages of devolution?

"And from what I understand, this wasn't unusual for Atlanteans, this flocking to the site of a disaster, this helping out. True?

"They had a tragedy themselves, I understand. Perhaps they are sensitized to this kind of thing.

"Anyway, from what I understand, they saved hundreds that night. *Hundreds*. Swooping up from below, pushing the people into the lifeboats. There were thousands of them in the area by the time it

was over, all these lights—they have lights of some sort, yes?— all these lights flashing. It has been put off to delirium on the part of the passengers.

"I've never believed that."

The last notes from the day that Larkin and Robinson discussed *Titanic* with the Atlanteans say this:

••− / •−−•−••• / •−•−−••
−•••−••• / −•••••−− / •−•••−
−•••••− / •−−•−••• / •−•••• / −
••••−−•• / •−•••• / −−•••−•−
•••• / •−−••−••• / −•••• / −•
−•−•−−••−•−•−••• / •

and this:

•−−• / −••••−•• / •−−••••
−− / •−−• / −•−•−•−−• / •
•−•••−•−•− / •−−• / •−•−•• /
•••−•−−••−•• / ••− / •
−−•••• / −•−•−− / •−•−−

••−−••••−•−•− / ••−−•••−•−−•
−•−−••−•−• / •••••−•−•••••−•−•−

which, deciphered, say, "It was awful, that night, as bad as ours, with the crying" and "We did what we could. We are sorry it was not enough. It broke our hearts."

*C*LIVE CUSSLER, avid bungee jumper, cigar smoker and deep-sea diver; founder of the National Underwater and Marine Agency; honoree of the Explorers Club (the Lowell Thomas Award for outstanding underwater exploration); author of a dozen ocean-oriented thrillers, including *Raise the Titanic!*, *The Sea Hunters* and the forthcoming *Atlantis Found*, books which have sold more than 100 million copies in more than 40 different languages, says, "We're letting them down. They've been good to us. We're not being good to them. I've seen some of them suffering, and it's simply not fair. It's not fair and it's not right."

Clive Cussler,
author
and activist

"I'm not saying it's anything specific that we're doing to them. It's what we're doing—gradually, generally—to our oceans."

Cussler is speaking by phone from his home in Telluride, Colorado. Again, as with all of the sources, I was directed his way by Atwater.

"Cussler is one of the connected people," Atwater said one afternoon. "There are a few of them out there who know all about this thing, and are trying to get something done on Atlantis's behalf." As he talked he scribbled on a notepad. He handed it over. "Here," he said. "These folks are currently working to stave off what looks to be an inevitable, inhumane, perhaps imminent disaster. Ask them what they're up to."

I looked at the list. Amos was another of the connecteds, of course, as was Explorers Club president Fred McLaren, our Knossos expert from way back. "Well," I said, "I've already talked to McLaren . . ."

"Talk to McLaren again," Atwater insisted abruptly.

***

AND SO IT IS that, several weeks after our first conversation, I return to New York City for a second meeting with McLaren.

Forthrightly, I challenge the distinguished gentleman: "You didn't tell me you knew of Atlantis."

"You didn't ask."

In his seafaring days, Captain McLaren enjoyed many reasonably close encounters with Atlanteans.

"I all but asked."

"And yet you didn't ask the question," McLaren says evenly. "Also, I didn't know what you knew. I didn't know who had sent you. Now I do."

"He told you about me."

"Yes, and he told me that you were nearly finished with your research."

"I am," I acknowledge. I want to tweak him; I want to find out just how much he knows. "Atwater suggested I talk with you again. Atwater has told me of people who have had contact with Atlanteans. Is this why he sent me back?"

"No," McLaren answers. "I have never made contact with Atlanteans. In the Navy I sailed all of Earth's oceans, but never made contact. I saw them, though—many times. The first instance would have been sometime in the 1960s. I knew the animals weren't manatees, they weren't behaving toward our sub as manatees would. There was a different kind of intellect at work, a hyper-inquisitiveness. They were scouting us, sensing us out. I had no idea what they were at the time."

Dr. McLaren had many friends at NOAA and at Woods Hole, and he started asking questions. It was Barbara Moore at NOAA who put him in touch with Atwater. "Yes, it was from him, the fellow you call Atwater, that I learned about Atlantis," says McLaren. "A few years ago he sketched some few details for me, and as he has learned more in recent

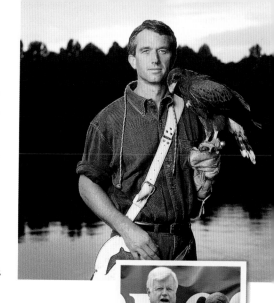

years, he has kept me posted. He has kept all of us posted—Cussler, Eno, that guy in Alaska and the one up in Boston, a bunch of scientists scattered about. He's got this little Atlantean network established, and now you're part of it.

"It's a crusade he's on, you know. He always wanted to make sure I understood what 'message' Atlantis was trying to send. He always wanted to make sure I knew of stresses on Atlantis, threats to Atlantis. His briefings were not merely informational, not at all. He wanted action.

"It's a difficult mission he's picked for himself, I'll tell you that. Atlantis's fate? I have no idea. There are big problems. I'll show you."

Dr. McLaren leads me from his office at the club into the even darker library. He takes a key from his vest pocket and unlocks a bookcase. He withdraws a large book and opens the cover. It's a fake; the inside has no pages, but is a hollow box. In the box are several folders stuffed with paper: reports, clippings. He hands me the box and says, "Spend just a little time with this. I'll be in my office."

Among the items I review are a 1997 study spearheaded by Dr. Andrew R. Blaustein, a zoologist at Oregon State University, that shows a close link between ultraviolet radiation (more of which is reaching the earth's surface as the ozone layer gets eaten away by the products of our passion for fossil fuels) and high rates of deformities and mortality among amphibians. Another study questions whether the effects of various El Niños were responsible for a 45 percent decline among sea lion pups off New Zealand. Florida's policies covering water use for agricultural and residential purposes are altering the salination of sea water and threatening marine life, according to a third report. A fourth indicates that decreases in the Arctic Sea ice cover caused by human-induced global climate change have had negative

impacts on a number of the region's marine mammal populations. In that 1998 study, published in the journal *Arctic*, Atlanteans are not specifically mentioned, but . . .

The "big problems" that McLaren spoke of are worldwide. Overfishing, pollution, global warming and who knows what other manifestations of the modern age have caused widespread depletion in many fisheries. The sea remains full of life and full of Atlanteans, but for how long?

"I wonder about that too, and so do my kids and my grandkids," says McLaren, as he welcomes

"I have no idea if we'll ever get this before the public," says Senator Snowe. "I'm not sure I should have brought Atlantis up at all."

me back to his office. "I called Olympia Snowe, the senator from Maine. She's a friend of mine and of Eno's. I told her about the environmental problems. She was very receptive. I went the extra step. I told her about the Atlanteans. I told her they needed help. She's trying."

Bobby Kennedy Jr. (top) stands ready to marshall his family's forces on behalf of Atlantis. Uncle Ted and cousin Patrick (above) could work the halls of Congress alongside Senator Snowe.

"I WANTED to get Dr. McLaren and others to testify, and they were ready and willing," says Snowe, speaking from her office on Capitol Hill. "Amos was willing to testify too. He told me that he was ready to come out about the Atlantis thing. He even said he might be able to get someone who worked at Woods Hole. He said he knew someone there with unique insight.

"But when I broached it here in Washington, they wouldn't even hold hearings. Everything was fine as long as it was technical stuff about pollution, stuff everybody could ignore because it would never

THE "CONNECTED PEOPLE" ARE TRYING TO SAVE ATLANTIS, LONG DISCONNECTED FROM POWER AND INFLUENCE IN ITS FORMER WORLD.

during a whale-counting expedition off Baja. "I was inspired to get involved," he says as he strolls the campus of Pace University in White Plains, where he teaches law at the Environmental Litigation Clinic. "When I was at one of our family get-togethers at Hyannisport last summer, I drove over to Woods Hole and asked some questions. That's when I met your friend. Quite a character."

"He is," I agree. "He is quite a character."

"He told me of Olympia Snowe's campaign down in Washington," Kennedy continues. "I know what she's up against. After meeting with your friend, I went to my uncle Ted and my cousin Patrick. They're ready to jump on the bandwagon if she can get something going. Ted could work the other side of the aisle for her in the Senate, and Patrick could work the House. But they were pretty frank, and told me it might be impossible to pull this off in Congress.

"I'd like to sue, but who? Here at the clinic we usually work against fresh-water polluters. With them, you can target not only industries but states and cities. With the oceans it's tougher. Which country do you go after first? Who owns the depths? Do we focus on global warming first or water pollution?

"I think what I'm going to try to do is get different stories moving in the press. A buddy of mine, Jay Heinrichs, is at *Outside* magazine, and the editor of *Outdoor Explorer* is another guy I know named Steve Madden. He's already told me that he'll run something about this.

"This could be a way to jump-start it. The media loves to feed off itself. It's my great hope that, a year from now, everyone on the planet knows about the plight of the Atlanteans."

make the papers. But when I mentioned the word *Atlantis*, bells and whistles went off. It was an absolute no-go.

"I have no idea if we'll ever get this before the public. Worse, I'm not sure I should have brought it up in the first place. Some people started to get antsy once Atlantis had been mentioned. I sensed a lot of whispering."

Efforts to aid the Atlanteans are bipartisan, as they should be. While the Republican Snowe is continuing to work for Atlantis in the halls of Congress—she will not be deterred—up in New York state the uber-Democrat Robert F. Kennedy Jr. is formulating plans for an offensive in the private sector. It is unsurprising that Kennedy, a lifelong outdoorsman and for years a crusading environmental attorney—foe of all polluters and friend of all fish—is engaged in this fight. He says he once saw a pod of very evidently beleaguered Atlanteans

I FELT that Atwater, after introducing me to Larkin, Robinson and Plummer, began to pull away. I'm not sure whether he thought that he had gone too far—had made some dreadful mistake—or whether he thought that his job was done.

Perhaps he sensed forces closing in. Maybe he felt that Amos, or even Sen. Snowe, could no longer protect him. Whatever it was, he was increasingly reticent about his role as coach, teacher, guru, sage. Atwater now seemed to be telling me that I was on my own.

And then, suddenly, I was. On a postcard-perfect mid-April morning, I arrived at the cabin to find a note tacked to the front door. It read, in part, "There's nothing left inside. I've taken the files. You've read all the important ones, and you've got your notes about what you thought was significant. Trust your instincts. There's nothing else for you to know that's truly vital, not at this point. You should realize: Larkin and Robinson know nothing beyond what they've told you already, and no one else at Woods Hole will add to the picture. Go with what you've got. Try to make sense of it, and do with it what you will—if anything at all. I trust that you know where the Atlanteans stand, and will not do them a disservice. I intuit that Amos was right about you, and I do trust you."

There was a check inside, and a postscript request: "Please give this to Pammy and Craig for next month's rent, with my thanks. Use the cabin yourself till June, if you like."

I DID THAT, and used the time to write this account of Atlantis that is now coming to its close. Before I sat down to that task, though, I called Amos.

"Where did he go?" I asked.

"Can't say."

"Or won't?"

"Or won't."

"Is he okay? Is he safe?"

"He's fine, and I suspect he will be fine. The folks at Woods Hole are paranoid, but they're not really dangerous—not like Atwater thinks."

"He went home, didn't he?"

"Can't say."

"I'll bet he did. I'll bet he's back on Orcas Island somewhere."

"Maybe."

"He used to talk about that. He used to talk, often, about going home. He seemed to be the kind of man who very badly wanted to go home."

"It's a theory."

"He always spoke well about the idea of going whence he came."

"He did."

"Amos . . ."

"Yes?"

"The island was his home, wasn't it?"

"What do you mean?" He was tentative.

"He wasn't . . . he wasn't one of them, was he?"

"An Atlantean? Don't be—" He stopped short.

"Amos?"

"Can't say."

"Or won't?"

"Or won't."

I NEVER HEARD from Atwater again. I walked out on the dunes each night of the forty I spent alone in Truro, trying to come to terms with Atlantis. I hoped, but never expected, that he would appear suddenly at my elbow and explain something else to me.

One night, when the moon was new, the waves broke upon the shore with a spectral phosphorescence, sparks flying into the night, dancing upward and evaporating against the black canvas, reaching up toward other stars—little ghosts, little angels. I wanted to comment upon that to Atwater. I wanted to ask if . . .

No more questions. No more answers.

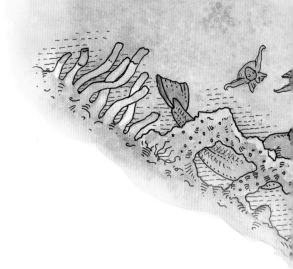

SWIMMING TOWARD TOMORROW
What Does Atlantis Mean to Us?

 OW, **AFTER ALL** that we have learned, let's consider—just for a moment—that the story of Atlantis is an impossibility. Never happened. Never could have. Let's ignore the evidence. Let's suspend belief.

It's not that difficult to do. A submerged race of beings genetically related to humanity is just as strange a notion as—well, as the opposite. It's like saying that we come from fish! It's like saying that our ancestors were not our grandparents, or their forefathers, or even the great apes of Africa, but were, in fact, microbial spores swimming in some anonymous swamp somewhere in . . .

Hello, Charles Darwin.

Okay, let's look at it another way.

It's like saying that a real, actual, once-great civilization can lie buried and undetected for millennia, nothing more than a rumor, a whisper on the wind.

And hello to you, the formerly mythical, now very real Helen of Troy.

All right. It's like saying that man can, or would, or should colonize . . . the moon!

And you think he will not?

Plato himself might have employed such a

method of argument and proof in the case of his dear, departed Atlantis. And he would have greatly relished the final part of the dialogue, which was, always, the lesson—the moral of the story.

What, finally, does it mean if Atlantis existed? If Atlantis exists?

It means three things principally, one of them far more important than the other two.

It means, most obviously—most *scientifically*—that Atlanteans have been and will continue to be resilient fellows. With each succeeding century, they have grown more adept at their undersea game. They have migrated and have settled new lands, in a peaceful way that is foreign to their above-ground relations. They have not only thrived and prospered as a nation, they have also grown increasingly munificent. They have benefited those outside their realm, even as they have profited their own community. They have grown strong in body, mind and spirit—individually in many cases, and as a collective always.

The existence of Atlantis means that human potential is at least as boundless as we now imagine it to be, and probably more boundless than that.

> THE EXISTENCE OF ATLANTIS MEANS THAT HUMAN POTENTIAL IS AT LEAST AS BOUNDLESS AS WE NOW IMAGINE IT TO BE, AND PROBABLY MORE BOUNDLESS THAN THAT.

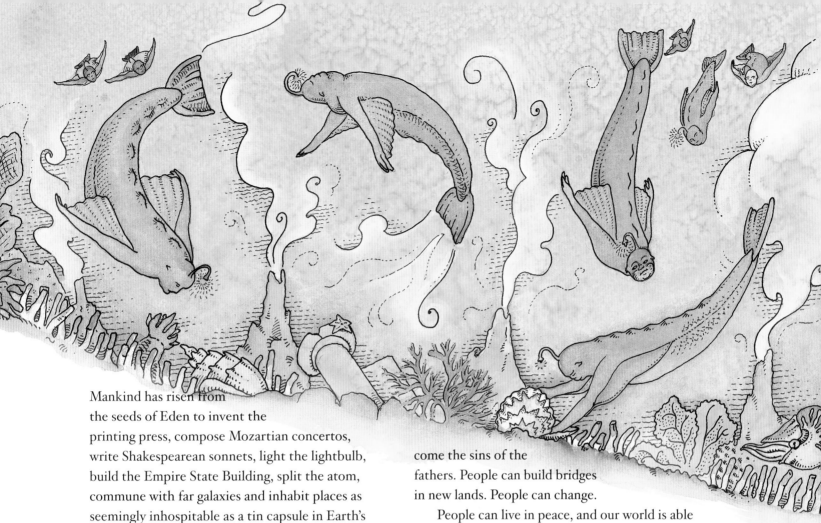

Mankind has risen from the seeds of Eden to invent the printing press, compose Mozartian concertos, write Shakespearean sonnets, light the lightbulb, build the Empire State Building, split the atom, commune with far galaxies and inhabit places as seemingly inhospitable as a tin capsule in Earth's orbit and a watery wonderworld in Earth's deepest depths. What's next? What could possibly be next?

THE EXISTENCE of Atlantis means, ultimately, that there are unseen forces at work in our world. And the existence of Atlantis gives a clue as to the nature and disposition of these forces.

The volcano gave the Atlanteans no time, no time at all. Their world vanished in a finger snap. Please understand: it's not that there was *little* time to act, there was no time. There was nothing that could be done.

But Atlantis was allowed to persevere. Something somewhere decreed that the history of Atlantis wasn't to be concluded in a way that shouted vengefully: Evil will be crushed! Evil will be eradicated! Case *closed!!*

Instead, this unseen power said, People will be given a second chance. People can change their ways. People can choose right. People can over-come the sins of the fathers. People can build bridges in new lands. People can change.

People can live in peace, and our world is able to let them live in peace. And if we go to other worlds tomorrow—in peace—then maybe there, too, we can live. We can live where we never thought we could. The world is limitless. It is bottomless and topless. It is a dark sea of unknown depth, and an endless sky of inviting, shining stars.

"There's a lesson in this," said Atwater, staring intently at the photograph, his eyes moistening. "It's a riddle. It's a puzzle. It's a test. I just know it. There's a lesson here."

Plato smiles.

FIN

Bibliography

Zofia Archibald, *Discovering the World of the Ancient Greeks*, Facts On File, New York, 1991

David Attenborough, *Life on Earth*, Little, Brown, Boston, 1979

Charles Berlitz, *The Mystery of Atlantis*, Grossett & Dunlap, New York, 1969

_____, *Atlantis: The Eighth Continent*, Putnam's, New York, 1984

Philip P. Betancourt, *The History of Minoan Pottery*, Princeton University Press, 1985

Andrew R. Blaustein, "Amphibian Declines Around the World," National Academy of Sciences, Washington, 1997

Mark Blum, *Beneath the Sea in 3D*, Chronicle Books, San Francisco, 1997

Daniel J. Boorstin, *The Discoverers*, Random House, New York, 1983

_____, *The Creators*, Random House, New York, 1992

Elisabeth Mann Borgese (editor), *Ocean Frontiers*, Abrams, New York, 1992

Bullfinch's Mythology, Crown, New York, 1979

H. G. Carlson, *Mysteries of the Unexplained*, Contemporary Books, New York, 1997

Rachel Carson, *The Sea Around Us*, Oxford University Press, New York, 1951

_____, *The Edge of the Sea*, Houghton Mifflin, New York, 1955

Edgar Cayce, *On Atlantis*, Warner, New York, 1962

George Howe Colt, "The Strange Allure of Disasters," Time-Life, New York, 1997

John O. Coote (editor), *The Norton Book of the Sea*, W.W. Norton, New York, 1993

Leonard Cottrell, *The Bull of Minos*, Grosset & Dunlap, New York, 1962

Ignatius Donnelly, *Atlantis: The Antidiluvian World*, Harper & Brothers, New York, 1882

Mike Donoghue, "New Zealand Sea Lion Dieback," SeaWeb, Washington, 1998

Arthur Conan Doyle, *The Maracot Deep*, Doubleday, Doran, New York, 1929

James Dugan, *World Beneath the Sea*, National Geographic, Washington, 1967

Richard Ellis, *Imagining Atlantis*, Knopf, New York, 1998

_____, *Deep Atlantic*, Knopf, New York, 1996

Arthur Evans, *The Palace of Minos*, Macmillan, London, 1936

Angelos Galanopoulos, "On the Origin of the Deluge of Deucalion and the Myth of Atlantis," Greek Archeological Society, Athens, 1960

Bil Gilbert, *How Animals Communicate*, Pantheon, New York, 1961

Stephen Jay Gould, *Dinosaur in a Haystack*, Harmony, New York, 1996

G.S. Haight (editor), *Essays and New Atlantis*, Van Nostrand, London, 1942

James Hamilton-Paterson, *The Great Deep*, Random House, New York, 1992

Graham Hancock, *Fingerprints of the Gods*, Crown, New York, 1995

Thor Heyerdahl, *Early Man and the Ocean*, Doubleday, New York, 1979

Charles Hirshberg, "The Tragedy of the Titanic," Time-Life, New York, 1997

Donald S. Johnson, *Phantom Islands of the Atlantic*, Walker, New York, 1996

J.V. Luce, *Lost Atlantis: New Light on an Old Legend*, Thames & Hudson, London, 1969

Charles MacLaren, "A Dissertation on the Topography of the Plains of Troy," Edinburgh, Scotland, 1822

Spyridon Marinatos, "Some Words About the Legend of Atlantis," Athens Museum, 1950

James W. Mavor Jr., *Voyage to Atlantis*, Putnam's, New York, 1969

_____, "Atlantis and Catastrophe Theory," Oceanus, Woods Hole, 1984

A. J. McClane, *Standard Fishing Encyclopedia And International Angling Guide*, Holt Reinhart and Winston, New York, 1965

George E. Mylonas, *Mycenae and the Mycenaean Age*, Princeton University Press, 1966

Margaret Oliphant, *The Atlas of the Ancient World*, Thunder Bay Press, San Diego, 1992

Mary Pope Osborne (re-teller), *Mermaid Tales from Around the World*, Scholastic, New York, 1993

Christopher Pick (editor), *Mysteries of the World*, Chartwell, Secausus, 1979

Nigel Pickford, *The Atlas of Shipwrecks and Treasure*, Dorling Kindersley, New York, 1994

Bradley Sheard, *Lost Voyages*, Aqua Quest, New York, 1998

Lewis Spence, *Atlantis Discovered*, Causeway, New York, 1974

H.R. Stahel, *Atlantis Illustrated*, Grosset & Dunlap, New York, 1982

Edward R. Tufte, *Envisioning Information*, Graphics Press, Cheshire, 1990

_____, *Visual Explanations*, Graphics Press, Cheshire, 1997

Jules Verne, *20,000 Leagues Under the Sea*, Miller and Walter translation, Naval Institute Press, Annapolis, 1993

Colin Wilson, *The Unexplained Mysteries of the Universe*, Dorling Kindersley, New York, 1997

DESIGNER: Emily Mitchell,
Nielsen Design Group

PHOTO EDITOR: Adrienne Aurichio

DIGITAL IMAGING:
Tim Nielsen/Badman

CREDITS BY PAGE:

6: Courtesy, Amos S. Eno/National
Fish and Wildlife Foundation

7: Courtesy, Atwater

8: Courtesy, Atwater; (Woods Hole)
Brian Smith/Stock Boston

9: Courtesy, Pammy and Craig Beaver

10: (Minoans) Corbis/Gianni Dagli
Orti; Nimatallah/Art Resource, NY

13: J. Carl Ganter

16: Corbis/Bettmann

18: (Lascaux painting) Corbis/Gianni
Dagli Orti; (Homer and Schliemann)
Corbis; (Lion Gate) Corbis/Hulton-
Deutsch Collection

19: Gustave Dore's *Minos, King of Crete*,
Corbis/Chris Hellier

20: (Evans) Corbis/Hulton-Deutsch
Collection; (Marinatos) Thomas J.
Abercrombie/NGS Image Collection;
(palace) Scala/Art Resource, NY

21: (vase) Scala/Art Resource, NY;
(pendant) Corbis/Gianni Dagli Orti;
(snake goddess) Corbis/Roger Wood

24: (Solon) Corbis; Raphael's *School
of Athens* (Plato detail) Corbis/
Vatican City

26: Corbis/Boston Public Library

27: Courtesy, Chris Benfey

34: Corbis/Ralph White; Corbis; *The
New York Times* (2); *The Washington Post*;
Courtesy, David Perry

35: Courtesy, Charles Officer; (caldera)
Corbis/Russ Ressmeyer; (eruption)
PhotoDisc, Inc.

36: (Chile, 2) AP/Wide World Photos;
(victims) Corbis/Reuters; (volcano)
PhotoDisc, Inc.

37: (San Francisco) Corbis/ Underwood
& Underwood; (Tokyo, 2) Corbis/Bett-
mann; Courtesy, George Howe Colt

38: (Lisbon) Corbis/Bettmann;
(woodcut) Culver Pictures;
(Voltaire) Corbis/Gianni Dagli Orti

40: (*London News*) Corbis;
(bomb) Corbis/Bettmann

42: (Hiroshima) Corbis/Bettmann;
(Chile) Corbis

44: (Donnelly) F. Gutekunst/
Minnesota Historical Society

48: Courtesy, Barbara Moore;
(snapper) PhotoDisc, Inc.;
(whale) James D. Watt/Masterfile

49: (Pliny) Corbis/Bettmann

50: Corbis/Wally McNamee

51: Courtesy, Mead Treadwell

52: Courtesy, Eric Widmaier;
(volcano) PhotoDisc, Inc.

53: Courtesy, Bil Gilbert (3)

55: (sculpture) Alinari/Regione
Umbria/Art Resource; (woodcut)
Corbis; (fish) PhotoDisc, Inc.

56: (sirens) Erich Lessing/Art
Resource, NY; (bathers) Corbis/Enzo
& Paolo Ragazzini

57: (Bosch) Scala/Art Resource, NY;
(woodcuts) Corbis/Bettmann;
Courtesy, James L. Gould

58: Courtesy, Amos S. Eno/National
Fish and Wildlife Foundation

59: (crab) Mark Blum; (toadfish) Tim
Rock/Animals Animals; (porpoise,
seal, manatee, orca) Bruce Coleman
Inc.; (scorpionfish) Joyce & Frank
Burek/ Animals Animals; (lobster, tur-
tle, angler, shark) Peter Arnold, Inc.

61: (Cousteau) Corbis/Bettmann;
(diving saucer) Otis Imboden/NGS
Image Collection

62: Corbis/Historical Picture Archive;
(Columbus) Corbis/Bettmann

64/65: Corbis/Ralph White

66: Corbis/Bettmann

67: Corbis/Underwood & Underwood

72: Chelmsford High School

73: Chelmsford High School (2);
Courtesy, Bruce Robinson; (reef)
PhotoDisc, Inc.

74: (Larkin) Robert Sullivan;
(diver) PhotoDisc, Inc.

76: Robert Sullivan

78: Robert Sullivan

79: Courtesy, Bil Gilbert

80: (jacket image) Gordon Gahan/
NGS Image Collection,
James D. Watt/Masterfile

82: (Verne) Corbis/Bettmann;
(*20,000 Leagues*) Culver Pictures;
(Cayce) Corbis/Bettmann

83: (Blavatsky) Corbis/Bettmann;
(Doyle) Corbis/E. O. Hoppe

84: Culver Pictures (3)

85: Photofest (2)

87: Courtesy, Charles Hirshberg;
Courtesy, Clive Cussler

88: Courtesy, Fred McLaren/
The Explorers Club

89: (Robert Kennedy) Andrew
Eccles/Outline; (Ted and Patrick
Kennedy) AP; (Olympia Snowe)
Corbis/AFP

ATWATER EVIDENCE
PHOTOGRAPHY: Brian Confer

JACKET IMAGES: Gordon Gahan/
NGS Image Collection, James D.
Watt/Masterfile; (Sullivan) Lucille
Rossi; (Wolff) Brian Confer

Acknowledgments

The authors would like to profoundly thank Emily Mitchell, Tim Nielsen and Jane Kowieski of Nielsen Design Group in Traverse City, Michigan. We would like to acknowledge the smart editing of Bill Rosen at Simon & Schuster and the hard work of Bill's colleagues Sharon Gibbons, Jackie Seow, Katy Riegel and Peter McCulloch. We would like to thank our agent at ICM, Sloan Harris, long a believer in Atlantis. Thanks go, as well, to K.B. Sutton, James Hagen, Dan Zemper at Well-Being Aquatics and Mike Spencer at Scuba North. Atlantis Rising would not exist were it not for the candor and truthfulness of our many experts and witnesses, and to them we extend thanks. For inspiration, we acknowledge John Michel, David Pelizzari and J Porter. For inspiration, tolerance, forbearance and love, we acknowledge our thoroughly water-weary wives, Luci and Carole, and our daughters, who, while amused by their dads, think their dads are nuts. —R.S. and G.W.

SIMON & SCHUSTER
Rockefeller Center
1230 Avenue of the Americas
New York, NY 10020

Designed by Emily Mitchell

Manufactured in England

1 3 5 7 9 10 8 6 4 2

Library of Congress Cataloging-in-Publication Data

Sullivan, Robert
Atlantis rising: the true story of a submerged land, yesterday and today /
by Robert Sullivan; drawings by Glenn Wolff.
p.   cm.
Includes bibliographical references. I. Wolff, Glenn. II. Title.
PS3569.U355A92 1999   813'.54—dc21   99 38765 CIP

ISBN 0-684-85524-0